WITHDRAWN

Viator

Other books by Lucious Shepard:

Novels and Novellas:
Green Eyes
Life During Wartime
The Scalehunter's Beautiful Daughter
The Father of Stones
Kalimantan
The Golden
The Last Time
Valentine
Aztechs
Colonel Rutherford's Colt
Louisiana Breakdown
Floater

Collections:
The Jaguar Hunter
Nantucket Slayrides: Three Short Novels (with Robert Frazier)
The Ends of the Earth
Sports & Music
Barnacle Bill the Spacer and Other Stories (AKA *Beast of the Heartland and Other Stories*)
Two Trains Running

VIATOR

A Novel by Lucius Shepard

NIGHT SHADE BOOKS
San Francisco & Portland

Viator © 2004 by Lucius Shepard
This edition of *Viator* © 2004 by Night Shade Books

Jacket illustration © 2004 by John Picacio
Jacket design by John Picacio
Interior layout & design by Jeremy Lassen

First Edition

ISBN
1-892389-44-4 (Trade Hardcover)
1-892389-45-2 (Limited Edition)

Night Shade Books
http://www.nightshadebooks.com

One
"...the husband of the linden tree..."

Wilander had grown accustomed to his cabin aboard *Viator*. Small and unadorned, it suited him, partly because his aspirations were equally small and unadorned, but also because it resonated with dreams of a romantic destiny, of extraordinary adventures in distant lands, that had died in him years before, yet seemed to have been technically fulfilled now he was quartered aboard a freighter whose captain had steered her into the shore at so great a speed, she had ridden up onto the land, almost her entire length embedded among firs and laurel and such, so that when you rounded the headland (as Wilander himself had done the previous month, standing at the bow of a tug that brought mail and supplies to that section of the Alaskan coast, big-knuckled hands gripping the rail and long legs braced, the wind whipping his pale blond hair back from his bony, lugubrious face, the pose of an explorer peering anxiously toward a mysterious smudge on the horizon), all you saw of *Viator* was the black speck of her stern, circular at that distance, like a period set between beautiful dark-green sentences.

The cabin was situated above decks. By day, natural light of an extraordinary clarity was filtered through the ports by sprays of broad palmate leaves, those of a linden whose crown had been compressed against the outer wall; and by night, illumined by a sixty-watt bulb above the sink and a bedside lamp with an antique tortoiseshell shade that Wilander had purchased from Arlene Dauphinée, the red-headed woman who managed the trading post in the town of Kaliaska, the cream-colored interior walls burned gold and the space shrank around him, conforming precisely to the sphere of his desires, secure and warm and secret, and he would have a sense of the cabin's light filtering outward through caliginous tangles of fern and vine and root, lending a teleological significance to the riotous growth, as if the forest would have no meaning, or rather would have the random, disorderly, terrifying causality of a nightmare were it not for this glowing cell encysted at its heart, occupied by its serene monastic dreamer.

At night the four men who had taken up residence aboard *Viator* prior to Wilander's arrival would visit him in his cabin, though this was by no means a frequent occurrence. Indeed, nearly a week elapsed before he spoke with any of them, having until then only caught glimpses of the others as they wandered the gutted bowels of the ship, and when they responded to his hailings diffidently or not at all, he had gone about his business, assuming they resented his authority because he was a latecomer, and that he would have to win them over with patience, by accommodating their eccentricities—yet on the sixth night, when Peter Halmus burst through the door, short and stocky, his muscles run to flab, his scalp shaved, his fleshy features framed to some self-perceived advantage by a carefully razored beard, a strip of dark brown hair approximately a quarter-inch wide outlining the jaw, with a thinner vertical line connecting the point of the chin to the lower lip, a conceit more appropriate to a nobleman of ancient Persia, the conversation did not proceed as Wilander had expected; which is to say, tentatively, pleasantly, building the foundation of a relationship.... No, Halmus spoke in a gruff voice, a voice atremble with anger, saying he had observed Wilander knocking out glass from a broken port and cautioning him never to do so again. *Viator*'s glass, he said, was his purview. He alone was responsible for completing a study of the glass and estimating its worth. He would tolerate no interference. And when Wilander, choosing not to confront the irrationality implicit in these statements, suggested that he had been trying to avoid an injury, nothing more, Halmus began to talk madly, mad with regard to his lack of coherence and also from the standpoint of a mad aesthetic, describing how twenty-two years of weathering unattended by any maintenance had produced discolorations that lent every crumb of glass a mineral value and refined mirrors into works of art; pacing between the doorway and the sink as he delivered this preachment, this rant, two quick steps, then a turn, punctuating disconnected phrases with a shaken fist, a slap against the thigh, his fulminant energy unnerving Wilander, who felt penned in his bunk, sitting with the top of his head just touching the underside of a shelf that held a few books, a wallet, keys, trinkets, coins, all he carried of the past.

 —Very well, he said. I won't remove any more glass.

But the glass, you understand.... It's not the important thing. We're to determine the salvage value of the metal. Isn't that what Lunde told you?

—Arnsparger is in charge of metals. This was said flatly, as if Halmus were stating an irrefutable law, an essential condition of the universe.

—Arnsparger, said Wilander

—Yes. The metal of the hull and superstructure. The rest, the fixtures, the galley, the engine...what's left of it. All that's Nygaard's responsibility.

—And Mortensen?

Halmus appeared to consider the question. Lately, he said, he's been preoccupied with the hold.

—Preoccupied, you say. Wilander swung his legs off the edge of the bunk and sat up. It seems you need little direction from me, but I should remind you this is a job, not a preoccupation. Lunde is depending on us.

—Lunde has no interest in what we do.

—On the contrary. He stated his interest quite clearly to me. We're to provide him with a estimate so he can decide what to do with this old wreck.

Halmus' face tightened in a scowl, as if he were displeased by the term *old wreck*. Shall I tell you about your relationship with our Mister Lunde?

—If you think it's relevant.

Halmus glared at Wilander and said, Relevant? What would you know of relevance? You've been here a week!

—I know I want to keep this job. Steady work, unchallenging work, with virtually no expenses. That's what's relevant to me.

Halmus lifted his right hand to his ear, palm outward, fingers curved, as if intending to hurl an invisible stone, and for a time he was incapable of coherent speech. Why should I talk to you? he said with disdain, letting his had fall. You're the husband of the linden tree. You have no speciality.

Several evenings later, Arden Nygaard knocked politely and inquired of Wilander whether he might be able to obtain a tool for the purpose of stripping chrome. He was slight and clean shaven, with limp gray hair and stooped shoulders, schoolteacherish in his wire-rimmed glasses, and yet he was possessed of a gaze so mild and unvarying, it gave the impression that he was simple-minded, dredging up Wilander's memories of dwellers in street missions and homeless shelters, men whose intellects, brutalized by poverty and alcohol, had been pared down to childlike proportions and who would happily stare for hours at a shoe or a stain on the wall, seeing there some delightful shape or a fantasy incited by that shape, and this impression of impairment, of gentle madness, was furthered by his response to the question, *Why don't you walk into Kaliaska and order the tool?*, which was, *I don't like going there*, followed by a prolonged nodding, as if he were serially reaffirming the statement, testing its validity by examining it from various angles, satisfying himself that its application to the matter was appropriate in every respect. Wilander thought to ask why he didn't like going to the village, but, suspecting that Nygaard would be no more incisive in his response and distressed by the presence of this sad little fellow who reminded him of a day not long removed when he had lived among such men and might himself have been seen as impaired by the casual eye, he sought to cut short the visit and promised that he would order the stripping tool the next time he went for supplies. Nygaard shuffled over to the sink and touched one of the faucets, petting the chrome, then smiled weakly at Wilander and went on his way.

Having had this much experience of Halmus and Nygaard, Wilander speculated that the other two members of the crew might also be mentally deficient, but Henrik Arnsparger, red-cheeked, round-faced, fortyish and plump, his belly overlapping the waist of grease-stained chinos, with thinning blond hair and an affable, garrulous disposition that seemed to fit within the parameters of normal behavior, eased Wilander's concerns; and when Arnsparger flopped into the swivel chair beside the tiny writing desk affixed to the cabin wall and let his burlap sack drop with a clank onto the floor and started in talking as if they were great friends who hadn't seen one another for a while, Wilander thought that here was an ally, someone in whom he could confide, someone who would give straight answers to his questions and not carry tales, and thus he asked Arnsparger to explain a few things: Why had Halmus called him *the husband of the linden tree*; what had he meant by saying that Lunde had no interest in the crew's performance; and why was Nygaard reticent about going into Kaliaska?

—You can never be sure what's going on in Nygaard's head, Arnsparger said. That guy's got no roof on his attic. Things fly in and fly right out again. But none of us like spending time in town. You've seen it. It's a horrible place. Drunks and snarling dogs and hostile stares. As for Halmus, I suppose he was talking about this linden tree. The one outside your port.

—I can't think what else he could have meant.

Arnsparger leaned back and blew out air through his lips as if snuffing a candle. Mortensen said something when I first arrived. We were the only two here, then, and he took me under his wing. He was a real talker in those days. Not so much now.

—How long has he been here?

—I'm not sure. He said he came when the snow was still deep. He's the one who set up the generators, you know. And he got the plumbing going, too. Anyway, he told me *Viator* had penetrated the forest and consummated a marriage between the organic and the inorganic. His words, not mine. I still don't know what the hell he was talking about. He said we were all part of the marriage. I was wedded to iron, he said. And he told Halmus he was beloved by glass. He's always going on like that. Spouting philosophy.

—It sounds more like fantasy.

—Is there a difference? Arnsparger nudged the burlap sack with his foot. What I'm saying, maybe he expanded the metaphor and told Halmus you were the husband of the linden tree. Halmus isn't smart enough to make something like that up. The guy went to college, but he don't have a clue. You should ask Mortensen. If you can persuade him to talk, I bet he'll have a hell of an explanation.

Wilander unscrewed the cap on a bottle of water, but

did not drink, puzzling over what had been said.

—It's an odd situation, Arnsparger went on. All of us have wondered about it. Doesn't it seem odd to you? Four guys...five, now. Five men of Scandanavian heritage down on their luck. They all seek employment at a temp agency run by another Scandanavian guy. They get to be friends with him and then he sends them to live on *Viator*. That how it happened for you, right?

—You were friends with Lunde? All of you?

—You thought it was just you, eh? That you were a special case? Me, too. I figured we'd be pals for life, me and Lunde. He bought me lunches, took me to movies, we talked about Sweden.... Not that I know shit about it. My family emigrated when I was three. For a while I thought he was an old fag, but eventually I decided he was just lonely, he wanted to reminisce.

—It was the same for the others?

—Yeah, but once we got here, Lunde wasn't so eager to talk to us. He keeps things businesslike on the phone. Anything to report? he'll ask. And you say, no...or maybe you tell him some bullshit. Then he'll ask if you've noticed anything out of the ordinary. Nope, not a thing. Okay, he'll say. Keep up the good work. God knows what work he expects we're doing. There's not a damn thing to do.

Wind stirred the branches of the linden, its leaves splayed across the port like simple green hands lovingly massaging the glass, and Arnsparger held forth on the folly of Lunde's plan, how ridiculous it was, the idea of bringing in forty or fifty men to break the vessel into scrap—you'd be deep in the red after paying for labor, living expenses,

VIATOR

all the rest. Now if *Viator* had reached her destination.... Had Lunde mentioned to Wilander that she'd been headed for South America to be scrapped? That's right. One of those places where shipbreaking is the main occupation. It must be a hellhole, wherever it was. And they must not care about cancer. These old ships, they were full of asbestos, every sort of poison. He'd done a computer search before leaving Fairbanks, at the public library, and the places where they broke ships apart, they were wastelands, long beaches with dozens of hulks listing along the shore, some reduced to skeletons, and hundreds of workers filing inside them, like prisoners marching into death chambers. In a place like that, breaking *Viator* wouldn't make extra overhead, and nobody cared how many people sickened and died as a result, not so long as they made themselves a few pesos. Here you'd have start-up costs. Nothing but overhead. You'd have unions looking at you. Labor do-gooders. All that for one ship? It made no sense.

Arnsparger pushed up to his feet, shouldered his sack, and shook Wilander's hand. Well, Tom, see you around. It's okay I call you Tom, is it? Thomas seems too formal under the circumstances.

—Tom is fine.

Arnsparger smacked himself lightly on the forehead. I almost forgot. He fished a cell phone from a trouser pocket and passed it to Wilander. Your turn, he said.

Wilander looked at him quizzically.

—We all took our turn, except for Nygaard, Arnsparger said. Making reports and all.

—Oh, right.

—I hate to put you to work right away, but can you order me some jewel boxes? Those plastic cases you keep CDs in? I could use a couple of gross. They're dirt cheap when you buy them in bulk.

—Why do you need them?

—For my samples. Come over to my place some night and I'll show you.

—I'm not sure I understand what you're saying about Lunde, Wilander said. It's your opinion that he sent us here for no real purpose?

—What can I tell you? When I call him, I always throw in some figures, some revised estimates. To keep him happy, you know. I like this job. But if I try to draw him out, if I ask about the project, when will the rest of the men arrive, or even just say, What's up? he either says he's got another call or that someone in the office needs his help. I used to think he was doing his pals a favor, giving us this easy job, but he doesn't act friendly anymore. Maybe he'll explain it to you. After all, you'll be making the calls now. You're the man in charge. Arnsparger grinned and threw Wilander a snappy salute. You're the husband of the linden tree.

Two

"...the queen of Kaliaska..."

Viator had come to rest in a nearly horizontal position, wedged into a notch between hills (a circumstance, Wilander noted, that lent a certain clinical validation to Mortensen's imagery of penetration and consummation), her port side braced against an outcropping of stone that had torn a ragged thirty-foot-long breach in the hull as the ship scraped past. An aluminum ladder was positioned at the lip of the breach, affording access to the ground. To reach the ladder, it was necessary to descend a many-tiered stair to the engine room, all but engineless now, a monstrous rusting flywheel lying amid bolts, wires, and couplings, the mounts and walls painted a pale institutional green, dappled with splotches of raw iron, and then you would pass through a bulkhead door into the bottom of the cargo hold. Light entered the hold not only through the breach, but through hundreds of small holes that Arnsparger had made in the hull with a cutting torch, removing triangular pieces of metal and, subsequently, storing them in jewel cases, and when the sun was high, hundreds of beams skewered the darkness with an unreal sharpness of definition, putting Wilander in mind of those scenes in action moves during which villains with assault rifles turn spotlights on an isolated cabin, a collapsing barn or the like, and fire a fusillade that pierces every inch of the walls, yet by some miracle fails to kill the hero and heroine, as if their true purpose had been to produce this dramatic effect.

Two days short of a month after taking up residence aboard the ship, Wilander descended into the hold, clambered down the ladder, and set out under an overcast sky for Kaliaska, where he intended to make a few minor purchases and hoped to spend the evening, and perhaps the following morning, with Arlene Dauphinée. Their friendship, after numerous long walks and hours of energetic conversation, had reached that awkward stage at which it would necessarily evolve into something more intimate or else plane back into the casual, and he was not confident that things would proceed as he desired, nor was he confident that what he desired was the best possible outcome—he had been without a woman for years, wandering from mission to alley to sewer grating, a world wherein the only women available were filthy, deranged, dangerous, like the young girl he'd befriended in Seattle, saved from the threat of rape and fed and otherwise helped, never once touching her, and then she had stabbed him as he slept because, she later told the police, his eyes had begun to glow, shining so brightly, redly, hotly from beneath his closed lids, they had irradiated the refrigerator carton in which they sheltered and set it afire—and he didn't know if he was prepared for the demands and stresses of an adult relationship; he valued the peace he had found aboard *Viator*, the lazy mornings, reading on deck under the linden boughs, writing in his journal about the ship, its curious crew, the woods, the sounds and sights of natural life surrounding him. And yet Arlene was unique. That was the only word for her; beautiful was insufficient a term, perhaps not an entirely applicable one, for her outer beauty had been worn down to the dimensions of middle age, her face whittled by years and eroded by the heart's weather, so that on occasion he thought of her as a figurehead supporting the bowsprit of a three-master, voluptuous and calm of feature, her core strength undamaged, but her paint faded, wood cracked by seas and storms. Even this minor stress, that created by the dissonance between his desire and his sense of security, was hard for him to bear, and he considered staying home that night, going into Kaliaska the next morning to offer her excuses, apologies, because he believed he needed a fresh start with her, another week or two to pull himself together, and then he would be ready; yet as he walked along the starboard side of *Viator* that day, passing beneath the linden, idly patting the trunk, he began to feel less anxious, less out of sorts, and though he did not reach a conscious decision, he soon left behind all thought of returning to his cabin.

The forest in close proximity to *Viator* was improbably lush, a micro-environment that would have been more appropriate to the Pacific Northwest. The black soil was carpeted with ivy, ground apple, and salvia; sword ferns sprayed upward from banks and hollows; mushrooms sprouted in gullies and beneath fallen trees; fungi and moss furred trunks and rotting logs; and, about thirty yards from the ship, a massive uprooted stump lying on its side, twelve feet in diameter, was so artfully decorated with lime green moss, it looked to have undergone an alchemical transformation—the dark circular underside of the thing, ragged with root fragments, some forming a witchy halo, had come to resemble those intricate reliefs depicting the Great Wheel of Life that embellish the walls of Hindu temples, only this particular great wheel was not painted in many hues, but done solely in green and black, and rather than illustrating the passage of a soul along the path of dharma, it presented a demonic version of that passage, a different course altogether, a far bleaker course complete with gnarled homunculi who appeared to have been banished, evicted, or otherwise brought forth from the emptiness at their midst, and whenever Wilander contemplated it—you couldn't just glance at the stump; it drew the eye in; it sent your eye traveling over the circuit of incarnations suggested by the twisted postures of the little root men and the ornate symbology written by flourishes of moss—he half expected to look up and discover that he had been transported to one of the stations of the wheel, a land ruled by an opal moon floating in a maroon sky where black dragons wheeled above spindly onyx towers. The nearer he came to Kaliaska, the less dense and diverse the vegetation; the ground cover melted away. After a mile and a half, the forest gave out altogether and from atop a brush-covered rise he could see the town strewn across an acreage of gravelly dirt the color of weak coffee: close by the shore, a handful of two-story buildings plated in beige-and-brown aluminum siding, one of which contained the trading post and Arlene's living quarters, another enclosing a beauty salon/barber shop, and a number of cubicle-sized rooms that were sometimes occupied by men from the freighters and fishing boats that stopped for supplies or were driven to anchor in the bay during storms; a swaybacked wooden dock to which a tug was moored; a gray beach with gray water lapping at it and a rubble of dark rocks jutting up from its southernmost reach; and, farther inland, more than a hundred small houses, many of the prefabricated variety, idiosyncratic in structure, but most of them white, with smoking chimneys, their unfenced yards littered by derelict cars, abandoned construction equipment, upside-down sleds and boats, doghouses, snowmobiles, ATVs. A couple of dogs were nosing along a deserted street near the shore, sniffing at debris. Parked behind the trading post were two state-owned yellow Caterpillar vehicles used for earthmoving and snow removal, and in each of their cabs, unidentifiable behind windows so smeared as to be opaque, someone was sleeping.

    Before Wilander arrived in Alaska he had imagined that Alaskan trading posts were uniformly rustic, dimly lit places with log walls, venerable wood-stoves, animal heads and antlers mounted everywhere, disorderly shelves stocked with soup, beans, rice, candy bars, fifty-year-old copies of *National Geographic* containing articles on the area, exotic locally prepared foodstuffs sold in mason jars, gutting knives, French soap, Russian pornography, bullets, whale jerky, slingshots made from fir and reindeer hide, whiskey, mukluks, sacks of flour, fish hooks, hard candy, fossil fragments, rope, fix-it-yourself manuals, work clothes, a few pretty dresses, canned moose meat, snowshoes, long underwear, ballpoint pens, native handicrafts of a surpassingly indifferent quality (carved ivory, paintings on bark, handmade dolls), an accordion, a guitar or two, dog muzzles, spark plugs, cooking oil, bongs, feminine hygiene products, grease traps, framed photographs of sunsets, paperback novels, animal snares...but though Arlene's TP (so read the sign above the door) stocked all the aforementioned items and more, there was no hint of disorder, everything shelved neatly and laid out in display cases, and the atmosphere was of a stripped-down functionality, not rustic charm, the fluorescent lights blazing, walls of unpainted planking, dustless floors, and instead of the colorful types Wilander had pictured sitting around the stove in his imaginary trading post, the only person present that afternoon was a long-haired Inupiat kid named Terry Alpin who helped Arlene out in the evenings and was standing by a bin of CDs, picking over the heavy metal section. Wilander asked him if that was his kind of music and, after a pause, the precise measure of which, Wilander had learned, was designed to convey contempt for white non-Alaskans moderated by a degree of respect due a friend of Arlene's, Terry said, No, man. It's for the seals. And when Wilander expressed bewilderment at this response, Terry said, The pups, man. Baby harp seals. They love the shit. You go down to the beach, hide out in the rocks with your Walkman. You slap on some Slayer, kick up the volume. Pretty soon the pups, they hear it, they come over to the rocks. You jump up and bash their heads in and get the skins. It's a lot easier than chasing 'em.

Viator

—You're serious? That's how you catch them?

Terry shot him a surly look. We useta stay up all night chanting to the seal god. This way, it cuts down on the brain damage.

—I thought the season...when they give birth. I thought that was in the spring.

—Just checking out some tunes for next year. Terry inspected the playlist on a Queens of the New Stone Age disc, set it to one side. I kept one pup alive from this last time and I been testing tunes out on him. He's getting maybe too old, though, to be reliable. The adults, they fucking hate music.

—Where's Arlene? Wilander asked.

—Out back. Selling some guy a flat of beer.

Wilander idled along a row of display cases, putting his nose close to one and peering at a grouping of men's rings with huge cubic zirconiums in ornate settings. He leafed through a fishing magazine that lay open by the register. He stared out the window at two men wearing jeans and denim jackets having a conversation in the middle of the street. He laid a dollar coin on the counter to pay for a Butterfinger bar, which he ate in three bites. I'm going out back, see if I can find Arlene, he said.

—It's your world, dude, said Terry.

* * *

Arlene Dauphinée's face was not a face that instantly drew men's notice. Unlike the hot color of a sign advertising a restaurant along a highway or the brightness of a lure dragged across the surface of a lake, it wasn't suited to serve as an initial attractor, to inspire certain hungers; at least she did not employ it as such. She wore no makeup, no jewelry. All her expressions, especially her smiles, were slow to develop, as if she didn't wish to reveal anything about herself, as if, in fact, she wished to deflect attention by minimizing her reactions, and when Wilander had first seen her, his eyes had skated away from her face, lingered on her red hair, clasped in a barrette behind her neck, the pale shade of red that often (as with her) accompanies freckly, milky skin; and then he had taken an inventory of her body, her slack, soft breasts, her slender waist and long legs, and it was not until their second meeting that he was struck by the astonishing composure seated in her face, emblematic neither of passivity nor of any quality that might imply resignation, but an active principle, a potent, ringing composure that signaled the type of person she was, a woman who hadn't been stranded in Kaliaska, stuck with the trading post because, say, her husband had died and left her in charge (she had never married), but had chosen this solitude nine years ago, this unsightly scar of a town on the edge of a thousand nowheres, because she wanted to live in a place where things were uncomplicated and self-sufficiency was a useful virtue, not—as was the case in much of the civilized world—a vestigial function, as useless as the stubby tail that briefly manifests on the human foetus; and once he had been made aware of this quality, he found it impossible not to see the unadvertised beauty of her face, the strong mouth and olivine eyes and lines of character that sketched a femininity considerably more alluring than that of the flashier, showier women with whom he had frequently become infatuated. She seemed a woman who might be someone's fate, who might be waiting patiently to perform in that capacity, and though he hoped she might be *his* fate, he was plagued by insecurity and prone to believe that what he felt was a foolish preoccupation, a form of desperation, or else a dream he was having about a subject that she was merely an emblem of—yet as they sat that evening in Polar Bear Pizza (which occupied half a house on the outskirts of town, the other half given over to a coin laundry), sharing a large double pepperoni at a picnic-style table covered by a checkered plastic cloth, beneath a painted wall menu with all the prices effaced that heralded, among other items, Our Stupefying Super Spicy Stromboli Sandwich, it may have been that her companionship shored up his self-doubt, for he suddenly felt that his business failures, the drinking and drugs and the vampire people with whom he had associated while he drank and drugged, the stages of the slow collapse that had led to homelessness...those things were behind him and he was ready to build on the wreckage, to address those problems that might arise with maturity and confidence.

—Living with such unbalanced people, she said, and paused to sprinkle parmesan over a slice. It must remind you of the shelters.

—They're not all unbalanced, he said. Arnsparger's okay. A little obsessive, maybe. And I've haven't talked to Mortensen yet... though judging by the way he avoids me, I assume he's not quite right.

—You've been here a month and you haven't spoken to him?

—Oh, we've spoken, but at a distance. We've said hello and waved. I've tried to catch him in his cabin, but he's never there. All I know about is that his beard and hair are gray, and he's thin. He did leave me a note a few days ago. Slipped it under my door. A note concerning you...obliquely, anyway.

—What could he possibly say about me? We haven't exchanged a hundred words.

—He seems to have a definite opinion of you.

—That's strange. Even when he was alone on the ship, he never talked to me. He'd come to the post, drop his list on the counter, and wait outside in the cold until I filled it. What did the note say?

—He said, Don't you think it's time you paid less attention to the Queen of Kaliaska and took your duties aboard *Viator* more seriously?

Arlene smiled. It's amusing to think of Kaliaska having a queen. Well, I've been called worse. But what's he talking about? What duties?

—I have no idea. Both Halmas and Arnsparger have told me they don't believe there is a job. They think Lunde sent us here for his own purposes. And yet they go about their days as if they're on deadline.

—Lunde?

—Jochanan Lunde. He runs the Manpower office in Fairbanks. He's the one who handed us the job. A nice old fellow. He treated me with great kindness. He treated all of us that way, apparently. Arnsparger said he originally thought the job was an act of charity. Lunde was giving us a place where we could rest and get strong.

—Oh, yes. JL Enterprises.

Wilander gave her a doubtful look.

—JL Enterprises. Jochanan Lunde. They pay all your bills. She sprinkled parmesan on a slice. So he's changed his mind about that? About giving you a place to recuperate?

—Maybe...I don't know. See, when I call Lunde—I call him weekly to give reports—he's very crisp. Perfunctory to the point of rudeness. It's like he's too busy to talk. Arnsparger thinks that he was only pretending to befriend us and he sent us here for a reason he hasn't explained. Me, I think Arnsparger was right the first time and it's more a case of Lunde's done what he can for us, now he's on to something else. Perhaps he's found someone new to befriend, someone he'll send to join us. Charity or not, I'm grateful to him. I'm glad to be here. Glad to have this time.

Arlene mopped up excess parmesan from her slice with a napkin, taking—Wilander thought—an inordinate time to do so.

—What are you thinking? he asked.

—If I tell you, we'll talk about it, and if we talk about it, it might make you self-conscious.

—I'm already self-conscious.

—Why don't you trust me on this? I'll tell you later.

—Maybe it won't be necessary.

—No, probably not, she said and laughed, two bright notes that reminded Wilander of the stairstep notes a soprano might hit before essaying high C.

—What's so funny?

—I was thinking how economical a little scene that was we just played.

He thought he grasped her meaning, but not being altogether familiar with her ways, he chose not to comment.

One of the two teenage Inupiat girls behind the counter, framed by a white arch on which a mural of polar bears romping across pack ice had been amateurishly attempted, sat on her stool and gazed glumly out at the tables, at two elderly women in blond wigs and anoraks and jeans sitting close to the door, speaking in whispers as they ate (a lesbian couple originally from Portland, Arlene said), and the other employee, a slightly younger girl, possibly the sister of the first, was leaning on the counter beside her and aiming a remote at a television set mounted on the wall above the tables, channel surfing—she settled on MTV, brought up the volume, and a faint music was heard. Arlene swallowed a bite and said, I can't picture you as an investment counselor.

—I wasn't a very good investment counselor, Wilander said. I probably shouldn't have majored in business. But at the time there wasn't anything I was passionate about. Might have worked out if I hadn't followed my own advice.

—That's what I don't understand—why you chose such a career in the first place.

—I thought it'd be easy money. What sort of career should I have had?

She tipped her head to one side, studying him. A landscape architect, she said firmly, and had another bite.

Wilander laughed, and when she asked what was funny, he said, I wasn't expecting a specific answer.

She shrugged, chewed. What will you do after you leave the ship?

—For work, you mean?

—Work. Yes.

—I'm not sure. I know I don't want another career. Nothing that'll make me crazy, take all my time. Just honest work. Simple work. Physical labor, maybe. I wouldn't mind getting back in shape.

The Inupiat girls burst into giggles behind the counter and Wilander, suspecting that he and Arlene might be the object of their amusement, glanced at them over his shoulder—they were turning the pages of a magazine with brightly colored pictures.

—You should eat, Arlene said. It'll get cold.

Though not particularly hungry, Willander devoured a slice in three bites, leaving the crust. Duty done, he gazed out the window at twilit houses and the dirt street and mountains in the distance with exposed ridges of black stone and snowy slopes, pyramids of white meat larded with black fat, and tried to think of something to say, something casual that would nudge the conversation toward a plateau from which they could gracefully ascend to the central topic of the evening, the topic he considered central, at any rate. His instincts with women, once sure, had long since been stripped from him and, his confidence beginning to erode, he worried that he was rushing things, that he had misjudged the moment. Everything he thought to say seemed overly subtle or childishly manipulative, and soon he began to worry that instead of rushing things, he might be letting the moment slip away.

—I may have some work for you. Arlene dusted a slice with red peppers, using her forefinger to tap flakes of pepper from the jar, taking great pains to distribute them evenly. The afternoon boat brought me a shipment. A lot of it's heavy stuff. Generators and TVs. I could manage myself, but I've got calls I'd like to make as soon as business opens on the East Coast and the boat'll be pulling out around seven. You'd have to start before first light.

—That sounds possible, Wilander said. I could probably....

—I can put you up. Be easier than walking into town at three in the morning.

She glanced up from her plate and engaged his eyes long enough to convey that this was both a functional invitation and a personal one.

—Okay. Yeah, sure, he said. I'll be happy to help you out.

Arlene smiled. I can't pay much, but at least it's not a career.

Three

"...an awful dream, terrible, not like a dream at all..."

Wilander's days lapsed into a pleasant routine. In the mornings he would sit on deck beneath the linden tree, encaged by boughs that overhung the rail, leaves trailing across his neck and shoulders, bathed in greeny light, hidden from all but the most penetrating eyes, and he would write in his journal and doze and dream, often of Arlene, with whom he spent his nights, walking into Kaliaska in late afternoon, and helping out with the stock until closing and then retiring to her upstairs apartment, which proved to be a place of rustic and eclectic disorder such as he had imagined the trading post might be, the rooms carpeted with Turkish kilims and throw rugs from Samarkand and prayer rugs from Isfahan, one overlying the other, and the furniture—secondhand sofas and chairs—draped with silk prints and faded tapestries, and on the walls were oil paintings in antique gilt or brass frames, the images gone so dark with age, they seemed paintings of chaos, of imperiled golden-white glows, gods reduced to formlessness, foundering in black fires deep beneath the foundations of the world, and only by peering at them from inches away could one determine that they were stormy seascapes and pastoral landscapes and portraits of aristocratic men and women in comic opera uniforms and gowns, all wearing the constipated expression that during the nineteenth century served as standard dress for the ruling class, and upon the end tables and dressers and nightstands were innumerable lamps, lamps of every description, bases of cut glass, ceramic, brass, malacca, polished teak, and onyx matched to shades of parchment, eggshell-thin jade, carved ivory, lace-edged silk, blown glass, and tin, yet no more than a few were ever lit at one time, and thus the apartment was usually engulfed in a mysterious gloom from which glints and colors and lusters of these objects (all gotten at barter from sailors, travelers, adventurers) would emerge, creating a perfect setting for Arlene, the rich clutter of a pirate's trove wherein she looked to be the most significant prize. These dreams were sometimes prurient, sometimes funny, sometimes sweet, and this heartened Wilander—the fact that his subconscious displayed a range of feeling toward her nourished his hope that the relationship would grow and become more than two lonely people having sex.

Shortly after he began spending his nights with Arlene, one morning as he lay on the deck of *Viator*, Wilander was visited by a dream that was to return to him again and again in variant forms. He had no presence in the dream, no sense of intimate involvement, being merely an observer without attitude or disposition, bodiless in a black place. Superimposed on the blackness was a tan circle, like the view through a telescope of a pale brown sky and what appeared to be five dark birds (always five) flying at so great a distance, they manifested as simple shapes,

shapes such as a child might render when asked to draw a bird, two identical curved lines set side by side and meeting at the point between them. Something about the dream, which lasted only for a few seconds prior to waking and seemed less a dream than an optical incident that may have been provoked by the sun penetrating his lids, unsettled Wilander, yet he failed to identify the unsettling element until the third recurrence of the dream, when he recognized that the winglike lines comprising the individual birds were not beating, but rippling, causing them to resemble flagella wriggling in a drop of water under the lens of a microscope. The bird things flew ever closer to the viewing plane and he came to suspect that their bodies might not conform to avian anatomy at all, but they were still so far away, they remained rudimentary figures without the slightest visible detail.

None of these dreams were of considerable duration, and though they disturbed Wilander, the disturbance was not so onerous as to distract him overmuch—far more disturbing was the demeanor of the men aboard *Viator* now that he had *hooked up with* (this being Halmus' appreciation of the relationship) the Queen of Kaliaska. Had it been asserted that he could be more isolated than he already was, that his shipmates might treat him with greater indifference, he would have pronounced the statement laughable and replied that the increment of indifference involved would be infinitesimal; yet he discovered that the atmosphere aboard ship underwent a marked chill, that Nygaard averted his eyes whenever Wilander came near, and Halmus no longer extended even a cursory greeting, and Mortensen ignored him completely, and Arnsparger's smiles were reduced to formalities, his chatter to ten-second assessments of the weather. Wilander classified their shunning of him as adolescent, the kind of wounded reaction that eventuates when a woman begins to dominate a young man's time and thus earns the resentment of his friends, of a group whose center he has been; but since the men of *Viator* were not young, not friends, acquaintances only in the strictest sense of the word, Wilander could not fathom the reason for their hostile reaction, nor could he understand the depth of his reaction to their coolness.

—To hell with them, he told Arlene. They act like I've betrayed them. Like we're fraternity brothers and I've broken the sacred bond. It's ridiculous.

Yet once back onboard the ship, he felt injured by their treatment and, while he had no intention of apologizing or placating them in any way, he sought them out, hoping that a meeting in a passageway or the hold or the galley would provide an opportunity for them to vent their displeasure and permit them to work past this problem and reinstitute the old, slightly less indifferent order. He made no discernible progress toward a rapprochement, but he came to anticipate the time he spent searching through the ship, because on each and every occasion he would stumble upon some fascinating object—for instance, a pale green section of the passageway wall outside the officer's mess where the paint had flaked away in hundreds of spots, small and large, creating of the surface a mineral abstract like those found on picture stone, from which (if one studied the wall, letting one's eyes build an image from the paintless spots, from scratches, dents and scuffs) there emerged an intricate landscape, an aerial view of forested hills—firs for the most part—declining toward water, and a large modern city beneath the hills that encircled a lagoon and spread along the coast, with iron-colored islands in the offing; or he might achieve a fresh perspective on some portion of the ship, much as happened when, standing in the engine room one night, he glanced at the relics of the engine and the many-leveled stairway ascending through the tiers and realized that this towering space and its contents had the appearance of a mechanistic church that had been violated and abandoned, its altar wrecked, its symbol of spiritual ascendancy rusted, littered with twenty-year-old trash: oil-stained cloths, bolts, shattered bottle glass, some of the railings loose, some fallen—and as a result of these dalliances, he found himself growing more intrigued by the ship, not curious as to its history, but fixated upon the beauty of its decay, the monument to dissolution it was in process of becoming.

    Three weeks after he and Arlene had initiated their affair, while sleeping on *Viator*'s deck beneath the low-hanging linden boughs, Wilander experienced a recurrence of the dream that was unlike any of its previous visitations. At the outset, all was as usual. He lay disembodied, in blackness, staring at the pale brown circle wherein the four birdlike creatures flew, still mysterious with distance, when one separated from the rest and approached with apparent purposefulness, as if it had noticed something of interest and were coming for a better look. It must have begun its approach from a good ways off—for what seemed two or three minutes, he could detect no change in its aspect, except that it proved to be a dark earthy brown in color, not black as it had appeared at a greater remove, and then suddenly it rushed upon him, or upon whatever dream-object it had noticed, and that simple shape of two identical curved lines resolved into two glistening, ropy segments of flesh, united by a ridged structure...and yet it swooped past so swiftly, he could not be certain he had seen anything of the sort, he might have supplied the details from his imagination to give form to what had been, essentially, a blur. Nor was he certain of its size, though he had an apprehension of enormity and tremendous power. Viewed at a distance, the bird things posed a far more unnerving image than had this fleeting close-up—their rippling stasis conveyed an air of horrid patience, the patience of carrion birds waiting for something to finish with death—but when he woke with his heart racing, he knew with a paranoid certainty that their waiting was done and that the creature had flown out of the dream and into the sky overhead and was wheeling about, preparing to make a second pass.

    He heaved to his feet and stood with his head and torso pushing up among the boughs of the linden tree, feeling more secure surrounded by greenery; but as he steadied his breath and tried to put the dream and his relation to it into a reasonable frame, through an aperture in the leaves, roughly oval, a lovely Edenesque frame itself, he saw a gaunt, bearded face like those portrayed by the ikons in his late Aunt Rigmor's collection, enshrined in a china closet at her home in Portland, a stately old house that he had hated as a child for its apparent fragility (he had been forbidden to touch anything), yet now recalled with inexplicable nostalgia—inexplicable, unless it were the ikons themselves that inspired nostalgia, for he had been quite taken with them and, curious as to their worth, their meaning, he had often stood on tiptoes and peered at them, as now he peered at the elongated, hollow-cheeked face of a suffering Swedish saint shrouded by matted shoulder-length gray hair, the waxy skin webbed with broken capillaries, and having a bladed nose and brown eyes as beautiful and profoundly sad as the eyes of a young woman disappointed in love, eyes that had registered everything essential about the world of men and had forgiven them their lustful natures, and a mouth all but obscured by a ragged beard that still showed here and there a few blond hairs: Mortensen. The shock of seeing him close at hand was nearly as disabling as the shock Wilander had absorbed from the dream, and he could think of nothing to say.

—Good morning, Mortensen said. Or is it afternoon? I often lose track. His voice was unexpectedly high-pitched and adenoidal, ill-matched to his appearance; its resonance made him sound a little like a boy trying to force his pitch lower in imitation of a man.

—Morning, I think. Wilander glanced up into the crown of the tree, trying to find the sun. Yes, it's getting near noon.

—Ah! I should have thought to look at the sky. I've been inside so long, my instincts have eroded.

Wilander became aware that Mortensen must be seeing him the same way he saw Mortensen, in a leafy frame, and the image this conjured, two men communicating by means of a weird organic technology, magical forest mirrors, made him chuckle.

—I'm not a social man, Mortensen said sternly. We won't have very many opportunities to talk. Perhaps we should make the most of this one and try to be serious.

—You have something to say to me? Say it.

—Only that we need you to be responsible.

—And what would you have me be responsible for?

—You spend most of the afternoons and all of your evenings with that woman. You sleep the mornings away and then you're gone again. How is that responsible?

—What should I be doing? Collecting scrap metal like Nygaard and Arnsparger? Pondering over broken mirrors like Halmus? Or would you have me haunt the ship like you?

—You're quartered in the captain's cabin. Surely that's an indicator of what you should be doing?

—So I'm the captain? Captain of a ship that will never travel another inch? I suppose I should be studying charts, plotting a course.

Mortensen made a diffident gesture. You're the one in charge, aren't you? You can hardly do other than determine our course. And then you have your reports to make. How can you make them when you know nothing of what's going on?

—I make the reports in a timely fashion.

—But what do you say?

—I tell Lunde the work goes well. Occasionally I throw a few numbers at him.

—In other words, you lie to him.

—It's what Arnsparger told me to do.

—Arnsparger! When Arnsparger made the reports, there was nothing to report. It's your job now and you need to redefine it. It's you who were meant to have the job when things reached this stage. To do the job correctly, you must observe what's going on.

—You're suggesting that I tell Lunde what we're doing? He'll fire us. If I tell him Halmus stands around examining bits of glass like a jeweler inspecting diamonds, or that Arnsparger and Nygaard cut little holes in the hull, in pots, in bulkhead doors...he'll have them committed.

—Those are the very things he wants to hear.

—How the hell would you know?

Mortensen's eyelids drooped and he seemed to be gathering strength through prayer. I was the first to come, he said. Therefore I'm the first to know things.

An image from Wilander's dream, the pale brown circle and the birdlike creatures rippling in the distance, floated up before his mind's eye. Unnerved by this, he was impatient to have done with Mortensen. It was early to be thinking of heading for Kaliaska, but he intended to do exactly that.

—If you know things before I do, Wilander said, why don't you tell me some of these things only you know?

Once again Mortensen paused before responding. You'll learn them soon enough.

—But I'm not ready for such knowledge now? It's too volatile, too alarming. I wouldn't be able to understand?

—Ridiculing me will benefit no one.

Wilander might have argued the point. Should I report

that to Lunde? he asked. That you have secret knowledge of the future?

—I see no reason why you should not.

—I've got a better idea. Since you've been here longest and know more than any of us, why don't you make the reports?

—I have my own responsibilities, Mortensen said. They require all my energy.

—Yes, I can imagine.

—Your duties are not so challenging as mine, but nonetheless they're crucial and you can't perform them in Kaliaska.

Angry now, Wilander said, These responsibilities that require all your energy, that are so challenging—perhaps you could explain them to me.

—There's a passage in the Bible that states one must be born again....

—I've had to pay for my dinner far too often by listening to that religious crap. I don't have to listen to it here.

—It states that one must be born again to enter the Kingdom of Heaven, Mortensen said patiently. I believe that's true of every significant passage.

—What are you talking about?

Mortsensen shook his head ruefully. Perhaps we'll speak later. I have things to do.

—What things? That's all I'm asking you! What could be so pressing you can't take a few seconds to tell me about it?

—It would take much longer than a few seconds, Mortensen said. And it would serve no purpose...not so long as you maintain your current attitude.

—Then convince me to change my attitude, Wilander said, but without another word, Mortensen stepped from view and did not answer when Willander called to him.

A bird chittered somewhere above, a patterned call that had the sound of a warning. Wilander glanced up through the leaves, trying to locate it, and was captivated first by the architecture of the tree, the axle of the trunk and the irregular spokes of the limbs, making it seem as if the linden were a spindle designed to interact in some fashion with the ship, and then by the uppermost leaves, almost invisible against the glare of the sun, and those just below showing as half-sketched outlines and a hint of green, giving the impression that the tree had not sprouted from the soil but was materializing from the top down, spun into being from a formless golden-white dimension whose borders interpenetrated with the world of men.

* * *

Walking toward Kaliaska, Wilander's frustration with Mortensen abated and he chided himself for having confronted the old fool. With every step, his mood was buoyed further by the prospect that in less than an hour he would be with Arlene, and by the beauty of the luxuriant growth, the sunlight filtering through the canopy to gild trembling leaves and nodding ferns, a feeling that peaked when, looking back, he saw *Viator*'s prow, black and made mysterious by ground fog, thrusting between two hills; but once he passed beyond sight of the ship, he was possessed by the feeling that the dream place into which he had gazed earlier that morning had a physical presence, a geography, and the ground whereon he walked was part of it, the firs, the mossy logs, and the carpeting of salvia and ferns, all of them were elements of an illusion that had taken root in the pale brown medium that enclosed the ship, growing there like fungus on a stump. The notion was, of course, irrational. He rejected it, he went at a measured pace, he fixed his thoughts on Arlene. But each step now seemed attached to mortal risk—at any second his foot might breach the apparent solidity of the trail and he would plunge into the pale brown void beneath and fall prey to the menacing undulant shapes that inhabited it. The certainty grew in him that a fatal step was imminent, that some dread trap he could neither anticipate nor characterize was about to be sprung. Before long, his uneasiness matured into panic, and, unable to restrain the impulse, he fled through the forest, soon forgetting what had so frightened him, afraid of everything now, of shadows and glints of light, of stillness and a surreptitious rustling among the bushes, stumbling, tripping over roots, scraping his hand on a stone, thorns pricking his arms, falling, scrambling up again, until he reached the rise overlooking Kaliaska and collapsed atop it.

    He had intended to catch his breath, then proceed to the trading post, but the town looked vulgar and forbidding in its plainness, the color of the dirt on which it stood virtually the same as that of the sky in his dream, the movement of dogs and people and vehicles conveying an aimless, annoying rhythm. Under the strong sun, Inupiat men and women trudged along the streets, some stopping to exchange a few words; a red pickup pulled up next to the trading post; three children played clumsily on the shingle, while their fathers patched a net. Wilander felt defeated by circumstance, stranded between two inimical poles, and wished he were back in the comfort of his cabin. He sat on a flat rock, flanked on one side by a bush with dry yellow-green leaves and on the other by the remnants of a fire and some charred fish heads upon which flies were crawling, and watched the sluggish creep of commerce with an utter lack of interest. Something was wrong with him, he decided. The past few years must have cracked him in some central place. His behavior was becoming as eccentric as that of the men aboard *Viator*. Not as eccentric as Mortensen's, but given what had just transpired, he doubted it would be long before he began collecting paint flakes or pressing linden leaves between the pages of his books. It seemed he had posed this—to his mind—overly dramatic self-diagnosis in order to provoke a denial, to energize himself, but it had entirely the opposite effect, weighing on him as would a criminal judgment; and, oppressed by the idea that he might be slipping, he sank into a fugue, staring at the town, seeing in its plodding regulation and drabness an articulation of his decline.

In the mid-afternoon, Arlene, wearing baggy chinos and a green T-shirt, stepped from the door of the trading post, shielded her eyes against the lowering sun, and peered at the rise. She spoke to someone inside and then walked toward Wilander at an unhurried pace, hands in her pockets. She stopped on the incline a few feet below his rock and said, Terry says you've been sitting here a couple hours. You okay? It was in Wilander's mind to assure her of his well-being, because she was intolerant of weak men, a by-product, he assumed, of a previous relationship; and yet she was also, if her depictions of former lovers were accurate, attracted to weak men—he did not want to think of himself as weak, nor did he want to play on her weakness for the weak or engage her intolerance by planting the idea that he might be on the verge of another collapse; but the way she looked, sensual and motherly at once, her breasts enticingly defined by the green cotton, a hint of sternness in her face, roused in him a childlike need for consolation. He caught her hand and pulled her down beside him.

—What is it? she asked, slipping an arm about his waist.

—I've just had a hell of a day.

She leaned into him, her breast flattening against his arm, and that yielding pressure was enough to break the last of his resolve, turning him toward confession.

—I've been having this dream, he said. It's an awful dream, terrible, not like a dream at all, really. It's more like a place I've been given to see. Hardly anything happens. But it keeps coming back and...I'm not sure what to make of it.

He described the dreams, focusing on the one he had dreamt that morning, and when he had done, she said, You need to get off that ship.

—I don't think it's the ship, he said, feeling an odd flutter of alarm.

—I wasn't talking about the ship itself. I'm talking about

the isolation, and those crazy bastards you're isolated with.

—I suppose you're right. But, uh...that's where I'm stuck.

—You could move in with me. On a temporary basis. Until we can find you your own place. That is, if you're planning to stay in Kaliaska.

Surprised, he said, That's very generous...and flattering. But Lunde wouldn't approve.

—Lunde! The way you talk about him, it's like he's your lord and master. Your Moses.

—He's been generous to me, but he's not my master. Just an old man who runs a temp agency.

—But what do you know about him? This is such a weird thing, this job! He may be using you for something illegal. A swindle, maybe. Maybe he's using your residency to establish a claim or...I don't know. It doesn't feel right.

—Whatever his motives, I need the job. And he specified that we had to live on the ship.

Arlene roughed up the ground with the toe of one sneaker and stared down at the furrow she had dug. What I'm saying, why don't you tell Lunde you quit? I can use you fulltime at the store.

—I can't do that! He said this more vehemently than intended and tried to compensate for his bluntness by saying, I'd feel I was shirking my responsibilities.

—You're starting to sound like the people you're complaining about.

—I don't mean my responsibilities to the job. If that were all it was, I'd move in tonight. You know that, don't you?

She sat with her folded arms resting on her drawn-up knees; a breeze moved some strands of hair that had been tucked behind her ear down to feather her cheek, and he gently brushed them back. She gave no sign that she noticed his show of affection, her eyes pinned to the trading post, where a group of teenagers on their way home from school, identifiable by their energy and the pink and red and turquoise packs on their backs, were jostling one another.

—The other men seem to be deteriorating, Wilander said. I'm worried what might happen if I leave.

—Are they having bad dreams as well? Arlene asked coolly. Is that a symptom of their deterioration?

—I haven't asked...but I get your point.

—Do you?

He slipped his left arm about her waist, the knuckle of his thumb grazing the underside of her breast. We're still trying to see whether we fit together, he said. You agree?

A pause, and then she nodded.

—I've wanted to say certain things, he said, but it was too early to say them. I'm not sure I have grounds to say them, given where I've been the past few years.

—You know that doesn't matter!

—But now, I think we've reached a point where somebody has to say something. You know, make a declaration. Would you agree with that?

—Yes...maybe.

—Well, I'm going to take a stab at it, okay?

As he talked, Wilander believed he was speaking from the heart, but at the same time he had the suspicion that everything he might say would become true and by giving voice to only a handful of potential truths, he was being effectively dishonest and thus, perhaps, obscuring the thing he wanted to express—this supposition was informed by the last occasion upon which he had spoken at length, when, coerced by the dictatorial priest who managed the North Star Men's Christian Refuge into offering public testimony regarding his devotion (completely specious) to Jesus Christ, he had experienced a similarly confusing interrelation between intent and performance, having brought a number of lost souls forward into the Lord's embrace, despite entertaining substantial misgivings about the benefits of Christianity to the disenfranchised. Yet as he talked that afternoon, telling Arlene that he wasn't arrogant enough to predict where the relationship would lead, though he hoped it would lead to deeper intimacy, to an unfailing union, his emotions fell in line with his words, or at least he no longer perceived so wide a distinction between them as he had during his impromptu sermon at the mission, and his tone grew impassioned, and he accompanied his message with caresses that, while intended to comfort and persuade, served also to inflame him. It was as if by admitting to love—to the desire for love, at any rate, since he did not mention the emotion directly—he surrendered to a thirst that had been half-wakened in him and now, thanks to his admission, was fully alive, fervently demanding. He wanted to be inside her, not later, but at that precise moment; he wanted to shuck off her chinos and sit her down on his lap and bury himself in the heat and juice of her, to touch her between the legs as they made love in view of the teenagers crowding together in front of the trading post, and was almost at the point of exploring her opinion on the subject—no one, he thought, would be able to see what they were doing at the distance—when Arlene lifted her hand, hesitantly, and touched his cheek. He kissed her fingertips, her wrist. It's not you making me reticent, he said. It's me, my lack of confidence.

—I know. It's just...I know.

—There's another thing I'd better tell you. It's really the most important thing.

She waited.

—I think you're hot.

She made a sputtering noise, an unsuccessfully stifled laugh, and shook her head vigorously, saying, I must be crazy! God!

—No, I'm serious. He grinned. You're very hot.

—Thank you. She composed herself and said, I haven't heard you talk that way before.

—Which way is that?

—Saying I was hot.

—It's Terry's influence. He's mentioned a couple of times he thinks you're pretty hot for an old babe.

—He said that? I'll have to give him a raise. She toed the trench she had dug in the earth. I guess you want to take things more slowly.

—I worry I'm going to have problems if I go too fast. I don't feel solid yet.

—Problems? Like...?

—The kind of problems that started me drinking. I don't want to fail with you. You don't deserve to have another wreck on your hands.

—Aren't you're running a bigger risk of becoming a wreck by staying where you are? Arlene rested her chin on her knees. Living on a wreck. Among wrecks. It's clearly affecting you.

—It's a challenge. But that may be what I need. And I don't have to worry about ruining things with you.

She was a quiet for a while and the shouts of the teenagers, as rancorous as the cries of gulls, filled in the gap. I have a challenge for you, she said.

—Oh, yeah?

—It's an urgent challenge. One that requires your immediate attention.

Puzzled, he said, Okay? What is it?

She gave him a soft rap on the forehead. You're a little thick today, aren't you? I was attempting courtly speech.

—I'm not familiar with it.

—I thought you were such a big reader! It's how knights and ladies flirted back in the Middle Ages. You know, the lady would say something like, Careful, sir, or you will prick me with your sword, and the knight would go, Could I but find the proper sheath, milady, it would do you no injury. And then she'd go, As it happens, sir, I have in my possession the finest and softest of sheaths, one that will never dull your blade. And then if he was having a bad brain day, like you, he'd say, You talking about sex?

—See, I heard no mention of swords and sheaths. That's what perplexed me.

—You're not perplexed anymore?

—Try me. Engage me in courtly speech.

—All right. Arlene appeared to deliberate. Why don't we go up to the apartment?

—Sounds good, Wilander said. I could stand a little sheath.

Four

"...I'm not sure what I'm seeing anymore..."

Though Wilander had no compelling reason to feel responsible for his shipmates, he took renewed interest in their comings and goings following his conversation with Arlene, as though his expression of concern for their welfare had not been—as he intended it—a flimsy tactic designed to reject, temporarily, her invitation, but a self-fulfilling prophecy with the dutiful properties of a vow. This adjustment in attitude had a minimal effect upon his relationships with the elusive Mortensen, the habitually surly Halmus, and simple-minded Nygaard, but it did strengthen the tenuous bond between him and Arnsparger. They had coffee together now and again, most often in Wilander's cabin, since it was the bigger of the two, and one evening, later than was customary, Arnsparger invited himself in as Wilander was preparing for sleep, bringing with him a cardboard box filled with triangular pieces of metal, each labeled and secured in its own jewel case; after urging Wilander to sit on the bed, he displayed them with a connoisseur's pride, offering pertinent commentary, and though Wilander was not surprised to discover that Arnsparger's samples had nothing to with the job, with evaluating the worth of *Viator*'s hull, he was astonished to learn that his guest's obsession involved the classification of (in a thoroughly idiosyncratic fashion) the varieties of rust.

—This one, now. Arnsparger opened a case and exhibited it with the panache of an upscale salesperson presenting a pricey necklace to a prospective buyer. This is *chian*. He sounded the name out—ki-ahn—and cautioned Wilander to be careful handling the piece; the flaking was extremely fragile. See how the metal appears to have effloresced. Here...and here. Like little arches. Almost a Moorish effect. And the blue...isn't it wonderful? I guess you'd call it peacock blue. It must be a nickel alloy. I got the sample from the railing outside the bridge.

—Why do you call it *chian*?

—The name just hit me one morning. It seemed to fit. He allowed Wilander to examine the piece a few seconds longer, then took back the case. Now here...here we have an example of *ozim*.

Ozim, a delicate overlay of black rust on red—like a Gothic lace, said Arnsparger; a scorpion's idea of beauty—was followed by *quipre*, which Arnsparger characterized as a piece of chiaroscuro, and that was followed by *shaumere*, *cuprise*, *noctul*; by *catrala*, *mosinque*, *tulis*; by *basarach*, *drundin*, *icthilio*, *ceranze*, and more. Seventy-three varieties catalogued in accordance with aesthetic criteria whose determinants were either too subtle for Wilander to perceive—though he acknowledged that many of the pieces were lovely, like miniatures wrought by a tiny, deft hand—or else were a product of dementia. After listening to a two-hour lecture on the elegance of rust, he was convinced

Viator

that Arnsparger, though more socialized than the other men, must be every bit as mad, and yet it was not the fact of his madness that dismayed Wilander, it was the effete, quasi-professorial air that Arnsparger affected while talking about his samples, a style that clashed with his usual bluff good humor and seemed incongruous coming from this overweight, slovenly fellow who looked less like an academic than he did a beer truck driver.

—You seem quite knowledgeable about art, Wilander said as Arnsparger packed away his show-and-tell.

—Me? Hell no! Arnsparger beamed. I know what I like. That's as far as it goes.

—But you're familiar with artistic terms.

—Oh, I ordered a couple of books after I started collecting. Maybe I picked up a few things. Arnsparger stowed the cardboard box beneath the wooden chair and took a seat. When I get home, I might do some painting. If I can get some technique down, all I have to do is copy my samples. They're a damn sight prettier to look at than most of the stuff you see in museums.

Wilander settled back on his bunk, plumped pillows beneath his head. What's interesting to me is that both you and Halmus have become artistically inclined while aboard ship, yet neither of you have any arts background.

—Huh! I hadn't thought of that, but it's a coincidence, for sure. Time on our hands, I guess. This old ship—he patted the wall beside him—it's got lots to show you, you take the time to check it out.

—Does Nygaard have a similar artistic passion?

—The poor guy imitates everything I do. He attached

himself to me when he first came and he's never gotten over it. So, yeah. He's collected a boxful of kettle tops and stove parts...that kind of thing. But—Arnsparger nudged the box with his heel—it's not the same as this.

—No, I imagine not. Wilander reached up and fumbled about blindly on his overhead shelf for a candy bar, located two Paydays, and offered one to Arnsparger, who said that his teeth were bad enough, thank you. From outside the cabin there came a long, thin cry, metallic sounding, that planed away into a whispery frailty—Wilander pictured a tin bird with gem-cut glass orbs for eyes, perched high in the dark crown of the linden tree, mourning an incomprehensible loss. What about Mortensen? he asked. Does he have a hobby?

—It's funny about Mortensen. There's times I think the guy's nuts, but he's too damn smart to be nuts.

—Intelligence is scarcely proof against insanity. The fact is, intelligent people tend to be more prone to certain types of mental illness.

—You couldn't prove it by me. I peaked in the fourth grade. Arnsparger chuckled. Mortensen, though...I tell you, crazy or not, he's a smart son-of-a-bitch. But he's not into collecting.

—Halmus told me he was doing something with the hold.

—Yeah. Usually he never stays with anything. He reads it and then he moves on to someplace else.

—Reads? What do you mean?

Arnsparger explained that Mortensen claimed the ability to interpret the ship through the signs manifest in its many surfaces. The rust and the glass, the raveled wiring, the accumulated dust, the powdery residues of chemicals—they were languages and Mortensen spent his time in mastering them, translating them. It sounds crazy, Arnsparger said. But when Mortensen talks about it, I get what he means. It's like with my samples. When I come across a good one...they're like these concise statements that pop up from the rusted surfaces. They come through clear, they seem to sum up what I'm seeing, what I'm thinking about what I'm seeing. Like with a slogan, you know. A decal or something.

—But the hold...You seem to be suggesting he has a special relationship with it.

—He spends a lot of time down there, writing stuff on the walls. But I don't know. He's liable to move on to something else.

Wilander pressed him on the subject of Mortensen, but Arnsparger, after answering a couple of questions, tucked his chin onto his chest, pushing his lips in and out as might a sullen child, his replies growing terse; finally he scooped up the cardboard box, surged to his feet and said he needed to get going, there were things he had to do, and when Wilander, bewildered by this shift in mood, asked if he had in some way offended, Arnsparger said, I'm fed up with you pretending to be my buddy so you can pick my brain. I'm not a fucking reference library! and stormed out, leaving Wilander to consider whether he had been insufficiently enthusiastic about Arnsparger's samples, or if the man's reaction was attributable to an irrational fit of temper, or if he, Wilander, had inadvertently crossed some impalpable boundary, one of many such boundaries for which *Viator* appeared to serve as a nexus.

The homogenous quality of the delusions that gripped the crew of *Viator* intrigued Wilander—although he had previously observed a sameness of mental defect among the men, not until his conversation with Arnsparger did he recognize how deep that sameness ran, and this gave him to recognize, in turn, that their presence onboard *Viator*, something he had theretofore thought of as a peculiar circumstance, might be a mystery of profound proportions. During his daily tours through the ship, in hopes of shedding light upon the mystery, he made concerted attempts to connect with Halmus and Nygaard and Mortensen—and with Arnsparger, who apologized for his flare-up, though he offered no excuse for it; but despite all Wilander's efforts, only twice did his contact with the men result in anything approaching an illumination, the first instance occurring one morning when he entered the galley, a room with stratifications of petrified grease darkening the ceiling and whose contents had been ransacked (whether by vandals or a rebellion against shipboard cuisine, no one could say), the shelves knocked down, a sink ripped away from the wall, the top of the stove—a black iron monstrosity blotched with rust (*icthilio*), but still functional—cracked, one of the oven doors missing, and there he discovered Nygaard cuddling a corroded saucepan in his arms, talking in a tender tone of voice, a hushed, consoling tone, as if the pan were a sick kitten that he was encouraging to suck milk from an eyedropper. Wilander asked him about the pan—what was its attraction, its point of interest?—and, receiving no response, pried it from his grasp, whereupon the gray little man fell back toward the door, gazing morosely at the prize that had been stolen from him. The inside bottom of the pan bore a whitish discoloration that resembled a ship ploughing through heavy seas, a similarity that seemed unremarkable until Wilander noticed that the overall shape of the ship was identical to the shape of *Viator* and a ragged dark line along the bow corresponded exactly to the placement of the breach in *Viator*'s bow. He suspected that the questions he wanted to ask were beyond Nygaard's ability to answer, but nonetheless he pointed to the discoloration and said, This looks like a ship, right? What do you think it signifies?

Anxious as a mouse, eyes darting this way and that, Nygaard retreated into the passageway. Wilander offered him the saucepan. Here, he said. I only wanted a look. But when Nygaard came forward to take the pan, Wilander hid it behind his back. First answer my question. What do you think it means? The picture of the ship.

Nygaard stared at a spot on Wilander's stomach, as if he were employing x-ray vision to peer through flesh and bone and see the pan. *Viator*, he said.

—This is a picture of *Viator*? That's what you're telling me?

Nygaard gave a tight little nod.

—Why do you think so?

—Because it's traveling.

—What's that got to do with anything?

—*Viator* means *traveler*.

—The name, *Viator*? Who told you that?

Nygaard's stare never wavered.

—Did someone tell you that's what it meant? Wilander asked. Who was it?

—Halmus. Nygaard stuck out his hand. Give it to me.

Wilander extended the pan, but kept hold of the handle when Nygaard tried to snatch it. What else did Halmus tell you? Did he talk to you about the ship?

—*Viator* means *traveler*.

—That's all he said? You're sure?

Using both hands, Nygaard wrenched the pan from Wilander's grip, but instead of running, as Wilander expected, he stood hugging the pan and said, I need some metal polish.

—What else did Halmus tell you?

—Metal polish, Nygaard said stubbornly.

—All right. I'll bring it tomorrow. Now what else did Halmus say?

—Promise you'll bring the polish?

—Yes, I promise. Now what did he tell you?

With the pan cradled in his arms, a crafty smile playing over his lips, Nygaard had the look of a husband who had been caught just as he was about to cook up his murdered wife's liver and thus no longer had any reason to hide the beautiful glare of his insanity beneath a humble exterior. He told me to fuck off, he said.

* * *

Several days later, as Wilander descended the stairs toward the engine room, he encountered Halmus, who was climbing the stairs, going with his head down, carrying a toolbox, and asked him what he had told Nygaard about *Viator*. Scowling, Halmus pushed past him, and Wilander, who—albeit taller and stronger—had previously been quailed by Halmus' temper, felt a burst of heat and hatred so all-consuming, it seemed to have been produced by a chemical reaction, the ignition of some volatile agent in his blood, a childish response buried beneath years of socialization, muffled by the practiced constraints of a business life, and—eventually—suffocated by reflexes born of poverty and failure and dissolution, by an appreciation of your own unworthiness that leads you to avert your eyes whenever an insult is hurled your way, and yet had never been extinguished, hiding like an ember beneath a board, waiting to be rekindled. He caught Halmus' elbow and slung him into the railing, which broke free with a shriek and went spinning down to clang against the floor thirty feet below, and Halmus, arms windmilling, teetered on the brink of a fatal drop until Wilander hauled him back and pushed him against the opposite railing and asked his question a second time.

—I don't know what you're talking about! Halmus struggled against Wilander's hold.

Goaded by the man's foppish beard and the contemptuous set of his mouth, Wilander knuckled his Adam's apple and said, You told him *Viator* means *traveler*.

—That's what it means, you ass! It's Latin! Didn't you go to school?

—The school I went to, we didn't learn faggot shit like

Latin! You know what I learned? While you were studying Latin and going to art movies and jabbering about political injustice in coffee bars, preparing yourself for a life of taking drugs? I learned statistics, cost accounting! I learned how to make a fucking living!

—Yeah? And how'd that work out?

Wilander forced Halmus harder against the railing. What else do you know about the ship? What did you tell Nygaard?

—I didn't tell him anything! I don't know anything! Halmus twisted his head, trying to see behind him. Let me go! The railing's loose!

Though tempted to push harder yet, Wilander shoved Halmus down onto a step and loomed over him. From now on, when I ask you a question, drop the attitude and give me a straight answer.

As was typical, Halmus glared in response, but the wattage of his glare seemed reduced. You're crazy, he said.

—That's your diagnosis? I better get myself checked out, then. Someone who goes around all day picking up little pieces of glass, you need to listen to someone like that when they talk about mental health issues.

Wilander noticed the toolbox, which Halmus had let fall, and picked it up.

—Be careful with that! said Halmus.

—Is there something breakable in here? Wilander gave the toolbox a shake.

—Don't...okay? Please! Halmus had lost all hint of arrogance.

Inside the toolbox was a dagger-shaped shard of glass

wrapped in an oil-stained rag.

—Put it back, Halmus said.

—Did you find another prize for your collection? Wilander unwrapped the shard, nothing remarkable, a piece of clouded mirror glass that gave back a partial reflection of his face, but as he made to toss it aside, catching sight of it at an angle that no longer reflected his face, he noticed movement on the surface and, upon peering more closely, realized that the apparent movement—it had to be apparent, he thought, caused by his hand trembling, a shadow misapprehended, something of the sort—looked to be occurring *beneath* the surface, as if the glass were not a mirror fragment, but a dagger-shaped aperture opening onto an overcast sky clotted with real clouds, storm clouds, grayish black and tumbled by the wind, and it seemed he was diving down through them; they went rushing past, blinding him for long moments, then intermittently affording a view of the ground far below through frays in their gauzy substance, an indistinct landscape of forested hills ranging a seacoast and, as his angle of descent lessened, like that of a flying creature flattening out over the hilltops, he glimpsed something ahead, an interruption in the flow of the forest over the hills, along the shore—buildings, perhaps—and then the mirror was ripped from his grasp and he was looking at Halmus, stunned and shaken, trying to reconnect with the feeling of triumph that had gripped him the instant before the mirror was snatched away.

—You saw something, didn't you? Halmus said, tucking the mirror into his toolbox. What was it? What did you see? Wilander had half a mind to wrestle the toolbox from him, to look into the mirror once more and identify what he had seen, yet he was unsettled by the triumphant feeling that attached to the sight; not a sense of accomplishment, of having overcome travail or succeeded at some difficult task, but an exultant relief such as might be felt by a gladiator who, having beaten down his opponent, was prepared to deliver a killing stroke; and yet that was an inadequate comparative; there was nothing in his experience or imagination to inspire this particular feeling, nothing that could have provoked anything approximating so unadulterated and fierce a joy, and he thought he must have been possessed by the feeling, or that he had taken possession of an entity whose emotions had no commonality with human emotion, with either the fleeting passions of an ordinary day or the desponds into which a man might sink, as with grief and unrequited love, but were symphonic in their scope, wider, deeper, and infinitely grander than his own. Halmus demanded again to know what he had seen, and Wilander, hearing frustration in his voice, frustration and, he thought, an undertone of envy, suggesting that Halmus himself had seen nothing in the mirror, or had hoped to see more than he had, decided not to respond lest by doing so he negate an advantage he had won, an advantage whose value he had yet to comprehend. Ignoring Halmus' protestations, he continued down the stairs toward the engine room, toward the completion of an errand, the exact nature of which he could now no longer recall.

Viator

The things he had seen in the mirror troubled Wilander over the ensuing days, but thanks to their singular character, he was able to dismiss them as aberrant, a symptom of nerves or some related complaint. He was less successful, however, in explaining away the powerful emotion that had attended his vision; it seemed to have stained his soul, adding a new, unwholesome color. He subjected himself to analysis, thinking he might unearth something from his psyche that, amplified by stress, could have produced such a sweep of feeling; but in examining the passages of his life, his unruffled childhood, his curiously blank adolescence, a period during which he had become, for no perceptible cause, alienated from everyone, friendless and unhappy (though not monumentally unhappy as were several of his more gregarious peers, like Miranda Alley, a brainy girl with whom Wilander had sex on one flurried, forlorn occasion, yet had been unable to persuade her to remove her brassiere, because—it turned out—she habitually slashed her breasts with razor blades; or Jake Callebs, a popular kid who swallowed an overdose of Xanax while sitting at the edge of the athletic field and died watching a pick-up soccer game, the green expanse blurring, his being curving up with the cries of the players and fading along the air; at least this was Wilander's overly romantic view of the occurrence) and given to long solitary walks, his mind not focused on any particular subject, merely idling, and thereafter the renewal of college, a vital rebirth, a burst of social interactions and diverse pursuits that continued on for a couple of years after graduation...in contemplating this, he felt he was pulling at a loose thread and unraveling the garment of self in which he had been cloaked until there was nothing left except blankness. That, he thought, was the dominant pattern in his life, cycles of hyperactivity and blankness, as if he were prone to unravel after having acquired a certain amount of experience, and he thought perhaps that same pattern could be discerned to some degree in every life, and what made you unique was no more than a handful of easily unraveled threads woven across a blank template.

The canopy of the linden tree was so dense that the leaves shielded Wilander from rain whenever he lay beneath them, but one Sunday morning a stiff west wind blew in off the sea, driving the rain sideways along the deck, and he was forced to retreat into the officers' mess, where he sat at a long table, drinking coffee, feeling submerged beneath the noise of the storm, staring out the open door at the lashings of the crown and gazing at the walls, hoping for a let-up so he wouldn't get drenched when he walked into Kaliaska later that day. Like the majority of *Viator*'s walls, those of the mess were painted green and the paint had flaked away in spots, hundreds of spots, creating a design of pale lime and brownish black from which, as Wilander's eyes moved across it, there emerged an astonishingly detailed image rather like one that might be obtained from the Xerox of a photograph done on a copier whose toner was running low, a landscape contrived of darkly etched shapes and blank spaces: it seemed he was looking from a great height between the tops of two firs, down across a forested slope and lower hills toward a circular lagoon at the edge of the sea; surrounding the lagoon was a considerable city. It might have been, he told himself, a variant perspective of the image he had noticed some weeks previously on the passageway wall outside the mess. The impact of this casual observation did not strike him at once, but when, after the span of half a minute, it did, he stepped out into the passageway to determine if the similarity was actual or imagined. He went back and forth from the mess to the passageway, comparing details, and it became clear that, although the image on the wall of the mess offered a more distant view of the lagoon than did the one in the passageway, there were too many correspondences between them to ignore. Each portrayed a large building with a humped roof, like a sports arena or a convention center, on the inland margin of the lagoon; and on the thin strip of land separating the waters of the lagoon from the sea stood a palatial structure, its uppermost floor a third the size of the floor below, atop which was mounted some sort of array; and there were also correspondences, he believed, between the two images and the forest he had seen in Halmus' mirror: not only were they were aerial views of the same landscape viewed from different angles, that landscape was in its hilly conformation, in the shape of its coastline, very like the forest that enclosed *Viator*, albeit more extensive and having a city at its heart.

Wilander was a realist, an espouser of statistical truth, a believer in coincidence when no better theory arose to explain the inexplicable, but his rationalism did not completely immunize him against fear, and the idea that the ship was showing him pictures, that it possessed the unreasonable power to do this, frightened him. He did not believe in ghosts, in the symbolic weight of hallucination, in magic, in extrasensory perception, in oracles (though once his Yahoo horoscope, pointed out by a girlfriend, an ex-Goth with lacy black tattoos columning her spine, a vine-like structure made of spiderwebs in which tiny women were trapped that evolved into a curious evil blossom spreading across her shoulders, had proved uncannily accurate, predicting that he would receive good news from a banking institution about a private venture on the day his business loan was approved); nor was he credulous about miracles or people who communicated with the spirits of the dead or those who had dreams that allowed them to divine the locations of the victims of kidnappers and serial killers—he was impervious to such claims, he resisted them with adversarial fervor, and while he found it difficult to sustain this denial of the supernatural in the face of Halmus' mirror and the pictures emerging from the walls, he managed after a prolonged study of the wall in the officers' mess to control his uneasiness, countering speculations as to what the pictures might be—views of another world, another dimension, the work of a poltergeist—with the notion that it didn't matter what they were; so what if a ghost was sending signals or the ship was coming alive or some more equivocal madness was involved, because nothing had happened, nothing bad, in all the weeks, the months now, that he had lived aboard *Viator*; and what was there apart from these piddling anomalies, anomalies that could well be supported by a logical explanation, one he hadn't fathomed yet, to suggest that anything bad would happen?

VIATOR

If a scrap of ectoplasm was acting unruly, an imp or spirit making sport, it didn't change the fact that he was healthier and more psychologically sound than he had been in years, that he had a woman who cared for him and hopes for the future. He set about tidying his mental processes, trying to sweep aside anxiety, but his cell phone rang, seeming to leap against his chest from the breast pocket of his shirt, and the superficial calm he had established was demolished. He switched the phone on and said, Hello, assuming it would be Arlene, but half expecting to hear a grinding tonality, the voice of the ship announcing itself for some grim purpose.

—Where are you? Arlene asked.

—*Viator*, he said.

—I know! I meant, why aren't you here? Did you forget? You were going to help me this afternoon.

—Not until two.

—It's after three.

—I've been waiting for the rain to let up.

—It stopped raining hours ago.

Wilander glanced at the open door. The rain had, indeed, stopped; the wind had subsided and the sun was out. I'm sorry, he said. I'll come right now.

—You sound funny. Are you all right?

—I'm just distracted. I've been...I was looking at something weird.

—Something weird aboard *Viator*? Who would have thought?

The detail of the forest and the city on the wall seemed sharper than before, as if the image were setting, like a print in a bath of developer.

 —So, she said. Are you going to tell me what's weird?

 —I don't know how to explain it. I...I'm not sure what I'm seeing anymore.

Wind swayed the linden boughs; the clustered leaves rustled and appeared to be spinning; clever, shiny green paddles registering the flow of light and air; the hidden metal-throated bird gave its long, declining cry. Wilander had an eerie feeling of dislocation, as if—were he to turn around—he would discover that the walls and the body of the ship had dissolved and he would see, instead, a forest, and, below, a lagoon and a city.

 —Should I be worried about you? Arlene asked.

 —I don't suppose it could hurt, he said.

FIVE
"...betwixt and between..."

When he called in his reports to Jochanan Lunde, as he did one sullen, gusty July afternoon not long after this conversation with Arlene, Wilander would usually take himself to *Viator*'s stern, where reception was the clearest. Approximately forty feet of the stern protruded from the forest, the ruined screws hanging like two huge crumpled iron blossoms above a shingle littered with weathered shards of trees that had been crushed and knocked aside by the ship's disastrous passage, and strewn with mounds of dark brown seaweed that Wilander, though he knew better, often mistook on first sight for the bodies of drowned men. Standing by the rail that day, he felt exposed, vulnerable to the open sky and the leaden sea, its surface tented by innumerable wavelets close to land, but heaving sluggishly farther out, making it appear that a submerged monster was shouldering its way toward the wreck, and he had to repress an urge to duck back under the canopy of boughs, because the view from the stern was menacing in its bleakness—it seemed that the treeline marked a division between a lush green security teeming with life and a cold, winded purgatory populated by crabs and shadows. He gazed down at the shingle as he delivered to Lunde a litany of partial estimates and hastily conceived plans, responding to the old man's terse questions, yet only half-involved in these exchanges; and so, when Lunde asked if he had noticed anything out of the ordinary aboard the ship, instead of offering his usual pro forma answer, distracted by a movement on the shore below and to the right of the hull (an animal, he thought; one whose coloration blended so perfectly with that of the motley pebbles and the shattered, silvery gray wood, he could not discern its shape), he asked, What kind of thing are you talking about?

Following a pause, Lunde said angrily, How can I answer that? I'm not there. I don't know what's ordinary for you.

—It's all out of the ordinary, isn't it? Living on a wreck's not what I'd call normal.

—It bothers you? It's becoming stressful?

—No, I'm not saying that. I....

—Is the job wearing on you, then? The solitude? If so, I can look for a replacement.

Wilander retreated from a confrontation. It's just that given the context, I'm not sure how to answer your question.

—Well, let me ask it another way. Lunde's voice held a distinct touch of condescension. In context of your experiences aboard *Viator*, using them as a standard for normalcy, has anything occurred that you'd consider abnormal? Anything unexpected? Anything startling?

Wilander would have liked to ask why Lunde wanted to know, what possible interest could such information hold for him, but he felt he had pushed the old man as far as he dared. Nothing startling, he said.

—Unexpected, then?

—Not really. There's been some...odd behavior.

—Which is it? Not really, or there's been some odd behavior.

The animal below cleared a cluster of wooden debris and crept across open ground, but its camouflage prevented Wilander from identifying it—it looked as if a portion of the shingle had become ambulatory. The other men, he said. They've developed hobbies. They don't interfere with the job, of course, but....

—I should hope not.

Wilander peered at the animal—it appeared to be smallish, about the size of a badger, and moved fluidly, albeit slowly, as if sliding rather than walking.

—Are you there? Lunde asked.

—Yes. What were you saying?

—You were doing the talking. Something about the men's hobbies.

—Right.

As Wilander described Arnsparger's passion for rust, Halmus' obsession with glass, the animal passed into a clump of ferns at the verge of the shingle, leaving him disquieted, and when Lunde expressed impatience with his recital, stating that such eccentricities were to be expected among men dwelling in solitude, Wilander, annoyed, no longer so concerned with placating his employer, felt inclined to elaborate upon the unexpected, to tell of his recurring dream, the pictures materializing on the walls, the mirror, the unseen bird with the metallic cry that hooted incessantly in the crown of the linden tree, this nearly invisible creature on the shingle (a porcupine, perhaps?), and the forest itself—now that he thought about it, wasn't such temperate growth so close to the Arctic Circle not merely unexpected, wasn't it implausible, impossible?—but before he could begin, Lunde said he had business to attend to and reminded him that they would talk the following week, saying he hoped Wilander would have something more substantial to report, and ended the call, his bluntness giving Wilander cause to wonder if he had misjudged him, if the kindly old fellow he remembered from Fairbanks had only seemed kind in contrast to the unkindness of the shelters and the streets. That question, and the question regarding the overall reliability of his perceptions, nagged at him as he headed toward Kaliaska, and, taking into account his reaction to the forest, reminiscent of the reaction he had displayed after his talk with Mortensen, a feeling of unease growing stronger with every step, a pleasant walk evolving into a nervous, hurried flight, stopping now and again to mark an unfamiliar cry that filtered down through the boughs, glimpsing furtive movement in the undergrowth, sensing enmity in a place that had often nourished him with its dark green complexity, he revisited the notion that his problems might not be due to business failures, to failures of character, but stemmed from a physical condition that provoked intense mood swings. Since his arrival, he had more or less succeeded in dismissing this concern; yet now the idea had resurfaced, he fell victim to it as though to a sudden onset of illness, a sweat breaking on his brow, his hands trembling, unsteadiness infecting his thoughts. He decided to turn back, but, realizing that he had come over halfway, he went forward again, going at an erratic clip, briskly for a minute or two, then pausing, detouring around a suspicious hollow, a forbidding bush, and when at last he left the forest behind and reached the rise overlooking Kaliaska, he felt ambivalent in his relief, like a sailor who has survived a disaster at sea and swum to landfall on a hostile shore. The streets were empty of traffic, pedestrian or otherwise. Smoke trickled from chimneys; a few birds circled above the dock, keening. Wind struck cold into Wilander. Something was wrong. The wasted town and the barren earth beyond testified to wrongness as might an unfavorable array of cards; the line of the mountain peaks graphed a feeble vitality and its decline. Weakness pervaded his limbs, tattered his thoughts. He imagined he was fading, his colors swirling, his form blurring, drifting on the wind. Somebody fired up one of the Caterpillars parked behind the trading post; a gout of black smoke gushed from its exhaust, and a dog that had been sleeping beneath the vehicle slunk away, casting rueful glances back at the rumbling thing that had disturbed it. As if this had been their cue, two paunchy Inupiat women in jeans and sweatshirts, their hair loose about their shoulders, stepped around the corner of the post, walking at an angle that would carry them past his position. One waved with a hand holding a paper sack, the sort that generally contained a pint bottle and shouted, Hey, Tom! He returned a wave, but he didn't recognize them. They veered toward him and stumped up the rise. Their chubby, lined faces seemed like those you might find on copper coins of great antiquity, well-worn images of glum, inbred, unlovely queens. He still had no clue as to who they were. They smelled of whiskey and that smell sang to the weakness in him. The heavier and older of the two had matronly breasts, gray flecks in her hair, a Seattle Seahawks totem emblazoned on her sweatshirt; she asked what he was doing standing there.

—Hovering, he said. Feeling a little betwixt and between.

—Don't tell me there's trouble in paradise?

He realized she must be talking about him and Arlene. I'm just pulling some things together in my head.

She held out the paper sack. Want a swig?

His hand twitched toward the sack, but he said, No, thanks. The younger woman, her sweatshirt sporting an American Idol logo, squinted at him; her lips were badly chapped and a shiny pink scar, at least a centimeter wide, roughly paralleled the curve of her right eyelid. Man, you look sad, she said.

The older woman gave a sardonic laugh and the younger, angry, pried the sack from her grasp. Well, he does! she said. Look at the guy. He's fucked up! She drank and wiped her mouth on the shoulder of her sweatshirt.

—I'm fine, Wilander said.

—It ain't love trouble, what do you figure it is? The older woman reached for the paper sack, asking this in a murmurous voice, not making it clear whom she was addressing, but leaving Wilander with the impression that the subject of discussion was of little consequence to her, and she felt compelled to placate the younger woman with a response, otherwise she might hog the liquor.

Wilander's instinct was to reiterate that he was not fucked up, not sad, but then he remembered the women—mother and daughter, Roogie and Cat by name, they ran the coin laundry on the edge of town, and were genial, hardworking types except on the weekends, which they habitually spent drinking. He suddenly perceived them to be wise fools, like drunks in a play, existential savants capable of delivering a profound commentary.

—The thing that's bothering me, I get these mood swings, he said. One second I'm okay, I'm happy, I'm going about my business, and the next I'm paranoid. I think it might be something chemical.

The women stared at him, perhaps surprised that he had confided in them, perhaps too drunk to understand what he had said, and then Roogie, the mother, gave her daughter a nudge and said, Sounds like your cousin Alvin. What the judge told him before he went to rehab. Judging by her baffled expression, Cat did not recall the event, and Roogie went on, About how he had a syndrome from his drinking?

—Oh, yeah. Cat squinted up at Wilander once again. Maybe you oughta cut back on the booze.

—I've been clean and sober for over a year.

—But you was a drinking man, right? Maybe you caught the syndrome, too, and it stuck with you.

From somewhere in the town came the flatulent noise of an unmuffled engine starting up.

—Sounds like Bert got his truck going, Roogie said.

Cat grunted. Big fucking deal! That worthless son-of-a-bitch never's gonna give us a ride.

—Well, he might if you was nicer, if you didn't call him names everytime you see him.

—You want me to sleep with him? That's what it'll take. I'm not gonna sleep with him just so he'll carry you around to wherever you want.

—Only thing I'm asking is you treat him like a human being!

—He ain't no human being! He's a filthy old dog who owns a truck! Why you want to ride with him in the first place, I'll never know. Damn thing smells like he sleeps in it.

Someone—the malodorous Bert, if Cat and Roogie were to be believed—began gunning the engine, racing it. The women glared at each other, and Wilander, hoping to steer the conversation back on track, said, I've been thinking my problem, the mood swings, they might have to do with me living on *Viator*.

—Bitch! Cat said to Roogie. What do you care what he does to me? He could knock my eye out and leave me crawling in the mud, that'd be all right 'long as he drives you over to Anchorage once a month.

—I should smack you for saying that! Hands on hips, Roogie faced down her daughter.

—Go ahead! Wouldn't be the first time!

—All I done for you, how can you accuse me of not caring?

—It seems I've always had them, Wilander said. But

since I came here, it's like moods that used to last for months come and go in a matter of hours.

Scowling, Roogie swiveled her head toward him. What the hell are you talking about?

Cat said, You done so much for me, how come I'm still living in this shithole?

Wilander decided to try another tack. Either of you ever hear any rumors floating around about *Viator*. Anything strange.

—I hear there's a buncha queers living out there now, said Cat.

—I don't know where you get your mouth, Roogie said to her. You didn't get that mouth from me.

—Naw, I musta got it from my *real* mother!

The engine shut down and, as though its operation had been tied in with the functioning of the weather, the wind died. In the quiet, Wilander heard waves slapping against the dock. There aren't any scary stories about the ship? he asked. Ghost stories...anything like that.

Cat scoffed at this. You seen a ghost, didja?

Wilander said that he had not.

—Then why you going on about 'em for?

Roogie put a hand on Wilander's shoulder, her expression a parody of sympathetic concern. Whatever your problem is, Tom, there's an easy solution. All you gotta do is do right by Arlene, and everything'll fall into place.

—How am I not doing right by her?

—Arlene's a good woman. You need to get off the fence and commit to her. You take care of her, she'll take care of you.

—A good woman don't charge six dollars for a pack of smokes, said Cat.

—That's the tax! She can't help that!

—Did Arlene tell you that? asked Wilander. She's looking for me to commit?

—She don't know her ass! Cat said. She makes up shit all the time!

Roogie folded her arms, affecting injured dignity. Matter of fact, I did talk to her. Even if I didn't, it's plain how she feels.

Cat took a long swig of whiskey, too long, apparently, for Roogie's tastes—she snatched the bottle back and lifted it from the paper sack to check how much was left.

—That guy who came off *Viator* after it crashed, Cat said, he acted like he'd seen a ghost. Walked around staring at shit and giving a jump whenever you come up on him. He was here for a day about...then they came got him.

—Like you remember! You were twelve years old! Roogie said.

—I remember better'n you! Cat turned to Wilander. She was drinking so much back then, she didn't know about the crash 'til a week after it happened.

—What guy? Wilander was startled not just by her statement, but by a recognition that, until now, he had only considered in passing what must have transpired with the crew.

—The captain. Roogie re-sheathed the bottle in the sack and had a delicate sip, as if she intended to ration the whiskey from that point on. I heard it was the captain.

—How about the rest of the crew? What happened to

them?

—He's the only one I know about, Cat said, and Roogie chimed in, Mark Matchett, that's the doctor we had back then, he told me the guy was telling some kinda wild story about how come he ran the ship aground, but wouldn't nobody believe him.

—Mark Matchett'd tell you anything to make your eyes get big, Cat said. So when he slipped his hand in your pants, you'd think it was all part of a story.

—I taken all your mouth I'm gonna take! You don't know nothing about me and Mark!

—I know he'd give you a wink and you'd drop to your knees! I musta walked in on the two of you a dozen times.

—Goddamn you!

—Him with his back turned, fixing his zipper, and you wiping your mouth off. Didn't take a genius to figure out what you was up to.

Roogie made to punch her daughter, and Wilander, trying to stop her, catching at her arm, sent her off-balance; she slipped and sat down hard, fell onto her back, somehow managing not to spill the whiskey, and, after giving him a look that went through quick stages of bewilderment, hurt, and rage, finally settling on despair, she began to sob. He bent to help her stand, but Cat pushed him away and shouted, Keep your fucking hands off my mama!

Wilander attempted to explain what had happened, but she screamed at him and Roogie's sobs escalated into a wail, as if she were encouraged by Cat's solicitude,

—See what you done! Cat shoved him hard in the chest and he reeled backward a few steps. You keep the fuck away!

Tears leaking from her eyes, she kneeled to console her mother, putting an arm about her, joining her in a community of grief that was founded—Wilander knew—upon no specific ill, but was informed by the sense of impermanence that tars the human spirit, the stuff that glues it to the flesh, a sticky emotional ground where drunks and addicts and other fools are prone to wander, mistaking it for evidence of a grand significance in their lives simply because it's something they can feel through their self-imposed numbness. She took Roogie in her arms, rocked her. I'll kill you, she said in a shaky half-whisper, as if the words were an endearment. Touch her again, and I'll kill you.

* * *

The wallpaper in Arlene's bedroom, a gold foil-like material with black bars of sheet music printed across it, clashed with everything else in the room, but so did each object in the room clash one with the others, and thus from a jumble of color and shape and function was yielded if not a harmony, then a discordant uniformity: a brass bed piled high with pillows and a wine-colored satin spread; a teak armoire hulking up at the foot of the bed, like a beast gloomily observing the activity thereon; curtains of Belgian lace that, when blown inward, reminded Wilander of filmy sea creatures gathering food from a current; a leatherette recliner nearly buried beneath laundry; candlesticks of brass and silver and crystal and pewter, oddly paired, no two alike; glass jars filled with agate pebbles; a dressing table of age-darkened cherrywood covered—as was every surface—with a dozen varieties of clutter, its mirror wreathed by a string of Christmas tree lights; the sixty-inch television set, a different sort of beast, sleek and blandly modern; clothes and books and shoes and change and magazines and toiletries scattered across the floor (Arlene had foresworn the art of housekeeping); and, on the bedside table, a lamp with a lacquered green shade whose dim emerald glow lent a transitory unity to these disparate objects, hollowing the night shadows into the semblance of a mystic cave, an underwater place where might dwell a sorceress who had removed herself from the world in order to master some contemplative discipline. You could not simply enter the room, you were absorbed by it, becoming an element of its dissonance, and Wilander had occasion to think that the decor might not be, as it appeared, haphazard, but rather was so designed to accommodate the haphazard collection of men who had slept there.

That evening, the town still awake, music from the Kali Bar (so named not due to any devotion rendered unto the Hindu deity, but because the owner and a hired sign painter had squabbled mid-job, a slight disagreement escalating into a feud as yet unresolved) squealing in the distance, he sat in bed and tried to sound out the melody of the wallpaper, whistling it under his breath—it was as chaotic as the room itself, a tune such as a child might produce while banging on opposite ends of a keyboard. Arlene, lying beside him, asked, What are you doing?, and, when he explained, she said folornly, as if the oversight were a sorry judgment on her, It's never occured to me to do that.

—You'd think the manufacturer would have used a famous piece of music, Wilander said.

—Maybe it is famous. The wallpaper's Chinese. Some Chinese music sounds all fractured. Atonal.

He shifted so he could lie propped on an elbow, looking down at her body, her belly and breasts pale and unblemished, but the rest of her, even the insides of her thighs, patterned with freckles, a patterning so heavy and distinctly stated in places, it made him think of a leopard's spots.

—What sort of music do you like? she asked.

—I'm not much of a music lover.

—You must like something.

—I don't mind music, I just can't relate to it the way other people do. He pointed out the window, indicating the faint music from the bar. But I like hearing it from far away. Even if it's just a bar band, it seems to promise something good.

After an interval she said, But when you get close, it's not so good?

Alerted by a fretful hesitance in her voice, he said, That's right. What I said...it's a metaphor for how I relate to everything, not just music. Places, people. At a distance they're fine, but up close—he made a sour face—eventually they become intolerable.

—Don't tease me!

—Weren't you trying to read that into what I was saying?

Another pause, and then she said, I know so little about

you. Most of what I know doesn't apply anymore. You don't drink, you don't work in finance.
—The last months haven't counted for anything?
—Of course they have. But ever since I've known you, you've always been going through some change or another. I've never seen you solid.
—I'm not sure anybody's ever solid.
—Solid's your term. When you said you wanted to stay aboard *Viator* awhile longer, you said you weren't feeling solid yet...or something like that.
—I was speaking about relative solidity.
—Okay. I haven't seen you *relatively* solid.

He laid his head on her belly, looking past her pubic tuft toward the freckles that spread across her the tops of her thighs, tiny brown splotches like, he thought, the remnants of an island continent flooded by a milky sea. He felt the heat of her sex on his cheeks. He studied the freckles, wondering whether—if he were to stare at them long enough—an image might emerge, as from the splotchy walls of the ship.
—Thomas?
—Yes.
—What do you want after you leave *Viator*?

The prospect of leaving the ship seemed silly for an instant, like the idea of unscrewing one's arm or building a house out of cheese, and he thought he must feel this way because his time aboard *Viator* had permitted him to gather sufficient strength and confidence to look beyond himself once again, to be here, now, with this woman, and to recognize her needs and his responsibilities toward her—it was daunting to (consider) doing without the perspective *Viator* had afforded.

—Is this something you have to think about?" she asked.

He moved up beside her and threw an arm across her chest. Not the way you mean.

She angled her eyes toward him, waiting for him to go on.

—Nothing's changed, he said. I want to be with you. If things were different, I might choose to live somewhere less desolate. But that's not a real issue.

—You haven't spent enough time in Kaliaska to know it. You only know the post, the pizza place, the bar.

—There's more? He chuckled, gave her a squeeze. Kaliaska has a secret life? A hidden culture?

—There's the people, for one thing.

—Oh, yeah. The people. I talked to a couple of the people this afternoon.

—You can't judge everyone by Roogie and Cat, especially when they're on a drunk.

—They're not the only drunks in Kaliaska.

—Certainly not. People drink, they do drugs, they fight. When the fishermen come back after the season, it gets worse.

Seduced by the smell of her hair, Wilander inched closer, sinking back into a heady post-coital torpor; he rubbed the nipple of her left breast between his thumb and forefinger. She stirred at his touch and he wondered what she was feeling—she was ashamed of her breasts, thought them too large and pendant, insufficiently firm, incompatible with the slimness of her body, and was at times discomforted by his attention to them, but he loved their soft, crepey skin, their heft, how they dangled when she was astride him.

—Why do you like it here? he asked.

—Because I know where I am. When I lived in Detroit, I was always confused about what was happening around me. Anxious all the time. Now I've been here for a while, I understand the same things go on in Kaliaska that went on back in the States. Detroit's just a big Kaliaska. People coming in from all over. The difference is, in Detroit I'd never think to talk to those people. I wouldn't want to, I'd be afraid of them. There were too many people. I couldn't get a feeling for them, and so I didn't trust them. Here the ships drop anchor, ships from everwhere. Japan, Russia, Norway. The crews come ashore for a day or two, maybe a week if the weather's bad, and they tell me about themselves. It's a richer life. And it's less confusing, less fearful. Everyone's so frightened down in the forty-eight. Maybe they're right to be frightened. Life is frightening. But here...Okay. She turned onto her side, facing him, earnest, one hand touching his chest. Sometimes when they wheel out the big TV at the Kali and show a movie, I'll be sitting there surrounded by thirty or forty people. Some don't like me, because we've had business problems or whatever; some of the guys like me a little too much. But I know what to expect. I'm not worried. Knowing where I am, having that clear a view...It gives me a freedom I never felt in the States. It allows me to appreciate the people around me in a way I couldn't before. And they're not all like Roogie and Cat.

—No, some are like Terry.

—Terry's a good kid. You have to get past the attitude. Look, I'll admit the range of people here isn't what you get in a city, but some of them are remarkable. It just takes time to see it.

—You're very persuasive, he said.

—Apparently not. I can't persuade you to come live in town.

She tried to make a joke of it, but there was an undercurrent of tension in her voice, and Wilander, recalling what Roogie had said about Arlene needing a commitment, found it strange that he was unable to give that commitment, because when he looked at her, he felt something that wanted to commit, something that once declared would bind them more tightly, and he saw the clean particularity of her spirit, her soul, whatever you preferred to call the light that flashed from her whenever the incidental clutter of her mind cleared sufficiently to let it shine through, the bright flash of her being, and he knew that despite the superficially facile nature of their connection, lonely man, lonely woman, there was something between them that seemed ordained, something he had encountered only once previously and then with a college girl named Bliss, Bliss Giddings, a tall, slender, quiet brunette who was studying to be an astronomer and was devoted to the poetry of Cavafy; poems that, when he read them to himself, communicated a haughty, defeatist sensibility, but when she read them aloud rang with a lovely sad romanticism, and everything was going splendidly for them, they were inseparable, intoxicated with each other, until one day she vanished without a warning, dropped out of the university and returned home, leaving him shocked, deranged, in agony—she refused to take his calls, refused every effort at contact, and he soon learned that she had married a wealthy businessman, a wine importer twelve years her senior, so no astronomy for her, no meteors, no pulsars, no distant suns, no erudite speculation upon whether the shape of the unverse, as recently opined, was similar to that of the Eiffel Tower, shattering the reality of those who had based their faith on the theory that it resembled a football, and there would be no hazy unfathomable astronomical objects named Gidding, no prestigious international conferences in Lucerne, no moments of transcendant solitude at the lens of Palomar, the cosmos spread out before her as if she were a spy for God, just lots of expensive grape juice; unless, to humor her, the importer, one Adam Zouski (the cacophonous sibilance of Bliss Zouski an abomination by contrast to the liquid asymmetry of Bliss Wilander), bought a telescope and placed it on the penthouse roof of the New York City castle where she was kept, allowing her to revisit her quaint, childish ambition; and years afterward, many years afterward, she began to email Wilander, gloomy, self-absorbed emails that professed love for him and dissatisfaction with her life, with her husband, a correspondence that grew over the months in intensity and frequency—they talked on the phone, spoke of getting together, made plans, shared sexual fantasies, yet nothing ever came of it, their plans evaporated, their fantasies remained unreal, the emails and phone calls stopped, and he still could not understand why she had left him; the reasons she gave were so flimsy, as if she herself did not understand, and though it wasn't until he met Arlene that he was able to put that episode in a drawer and lock it away, though he recognized how rare it was to feel this close to someone, the only way he could think to explain his reticence about moving into town, an explanation that would have a tired ring to Arlene's ears, was that he was not yet secure in himself, not yet solid. Finally, without attempting explanation, he told her that however the job was going, he would come to her after a month or so, when the first snow fell, early September at the latest. She said, All right, but she wasn't pleased; he could tell as much from the compression of her lips, the deepening of a frown line, and recognized that his indecisiveness (that, he knew, was how she perceived it) bordered on rejection, and might be more painful for her than rejection. He started to offer an apology, but knew it would sound inadequate.

—I don't get it. I don't get any part of it. This Lunde gives you a meaningless job, and you.... She made a fuming noise and turned her back to him. What do you know about this guy? Nothing! You don't have the slightest idea what he's up to!

—It's only a month, he said, pressing himself against her from behind. A month! That's no time at all.

He continued to reassure her, kissing the nape of her neck, touching her breasts; and, his erection restored, he started to push inside her, but she restrained him, twisted her head about so she could see his face, and said, I don't want this to be an affair! Don't move in unless you love me! And that was the perfect moment for a declaration. She was inviting him to declare himself, making such a declaration easy, an informality, and he felt the words and the will to say them taking shape; but then she opened her legs and, as he glided into her—that's how it felt, a glide, like the splashless slipping of a diver into a medium wherein his weight was taken away, his thoughts stripped by the purity of entry, not only his flesh but also his mind immersed, drenched in her—all he managed to say, more an expulsion of breath than a commitment, was, I won't.

Six

"...a fifth season..."

During August, it appeared that *Viator* was being transformed into an enormous museum devoted to the works of a single artist, one possessed of an obsessively monocular vision, a fabricator of duotone vistas, pale green and dark iron, featuring a shoreline city and a forest. Every viable wall aboard ship was producing such an image and Wilander was initially disposed to believe this was a consequence of a perceptual bias that—as with the paranoia he felt while walking into town—stemmed from a chemical imbalance; but as the flaking walls of the passageways and cabins yielded their variant perspectives on the scene displayed upon the wall of the officers' mess, he found himself less interested in why they had manifested than in what they might represent, and undertook to create a composite map of the region portrayed, treating the forest and the city as if they were real. He thought to ask the other men to verify that the images were there, but August was not the best of months for relationships amongst the crew: Mortensen was rarely to be found; Nygaard, as had been his habit since their set-to in the galley, scurried away whenever Wilander approached; Arnsparger grew uncommunicative and truculent; Halmus stalked about the ship, his customary arrogance swollen to the proportions of hauteur, and responded to Wilander's conversational openings with imperious stares, refusing to speak, as if he were rehearsing for a role as a pharaoh or a headwaiter. For his own part, Wilander felt no great urge to communicate; he was absorbed by his new passion, snapping photographs of the walls with throwaway cameras he bought from Arlene, assembling the prints into a montage on the dining table in the mess, and painstakingly sketching from these materials maps of a nameless country (he attempted to name it, but the names he chose—North Calambay, Skiivancia, Vidoria, Alta Marone—failed to resonate with his nebulous conception of the place) that was very like *Viator*'s forest, just larger, hillier, and with more prominent landmarks. Not that he possessed comprehensive knowledge of his surroundings; he was only familiar with the trail leading into town, yet he perceived these distinctions in the same way you intrinsically understand the conformation of a room in which you're sitting, and that sense, that effortless apprehension of two environments, one immediate, one imminent (that was how he thought of the nameless country, as imminent, something on the horizon, a landfall not yet sighted) led him to surmise that *Viator*'s mystery was emblematized by its name, Traveler, and that the ship had been frozen mid-voyage, like the *Viator*-shaped stain on the bottom of the pot Nygaard had exhumed from the vandalized galley, and was straining to continue on its journey. That conjecture steered him once again toward the idea that his fixation upon the walls was akin to the dementias that afflicted the other men, that he would soon, if he had not already, equal them in madness, and yet, if he were to accept that prognosis, did it not suggest that Halmus, Arnsparger and Nygaard were seeing comparable vistas in their collections of glass and rust and scrap metal, and that Mortensen's ability—as Arnsparger phrased it—to interpret *Viator* through its many surfaces also allowed him to envision a forest and a city. And what did that suggest? At one point Wilander went in search of Halmus and Arnsparger, determined to learn what they saw, what they knew, what they felt; but when they rebuffed him, he did not chase after them. He was beginning to understand the reason behind their unwillingness to talk: though compelled by the mystery of *Viator*, they were not altogether eager to solve it; they were afraid that what they had gleaned concerning the ship's murky potentials might be true and thus did not care to validate as fact what was for the moment merely a suspicion.

Day by day, fear became increasingly dominant in Wilander's life. His recurring dream unsettled him and the act of walking through the forest into town demanded that he steel his nerves, for everywhere he turned, he spotted evidence of movement in the undergrowth, stirring ferns, disturbed leaves, and he believed these signs were not due to wind or the scuttlings of ordinary animals, but to the passage of creatures similar to the one he had watched from the stern while talking to Lunde, sluggish translucent beasts native to another forest, another coast, to a metropolitan Kaliaska encircling a lagoon and separated from the town he knew by an imperceptible and indefinable barrier. The bird with the metal throat kept up its keening; indeed, Wilander became convinced that more than a single bird was responsible, since those declining, dolorous cries now sounded throughout the forest, and he thought that the original bird had, upon finding a suitable roost, summoned its fellows and they had proved to be a reclusive species who nested one to a tree and whose solitary calls were designed to provoke no answer, like a sentry's announcement of all clear. Unnerved by these thoughts, by his almost casual embrace of their patent irrationality, he debated whether he should give up his job; scarcely a day passed when he did not entertain the idea—it had served him for a time, but now *Viator* had begun to unhinge him, to terrify him. During a mild yet persistent anxiety attack, one that lasted for several hours, he decided to visit Arlene, but was unable to bring himself to endure the suffocating grip of the hold, the hold where Mortensen muttered to himself and scribbled things, lending the darkness there a Cabalistic weight, and so he was forced to lash a length of rope to the railing near the stern, a spot beneath which the crest of a massive boulder lay fifteen feet below, and to descend to solid ground in that fashion. Each time he went into Kaliaska, he would decide that he'd had enough, he would send Terry out to collect his clothes, his books; yet his fascination with the ship drew him back. It was not just the walls, the half-glimpsed animals, and the birds that compelled him. Gazing at a fitting or a corroded hinge, at any portion of the ship, although he could measure no appreciable difference from how these things looked one day to the next, he understood that a deeper change was taking place in *Viator*; and, on one particularly stifling afternoon, as he paused to wipe his brow beside a bulkhead door, a bulging oval with a bar handle, studded with bolts, its green paint scarred and incised with initials, like a hideous iron blister, something that might have developed upon the hindquarters of a mechanical beast, it occurred to him—a thought that seemed a direct result of his study of the door, as if he were tuning in its vibrations—that *Viator* was not, as might be intimated, experiencing an awakening or an enlivening (the ship, to his mind, had always been alive, its vitality evident at first sight, its energy spilling out to nourish the improbable forest that formed its nest), but that it was moving; that, though engineless, *Viator*, by means of some imponderable process and through some unfathomable medium, was shifting closer to that other forest, the natural habitat of the metal-throated birds, close enough so their cries could be heard, and yet they remained invisible because the ship had not succeeded in physically penetrating their habitat. Informed by this insight, this hallucination, this fantastic narrative skeleton that could only have been constructed by an ex-drunk, ex-addict whose mind, after years of abuse, the penultimate symptom of which was the narrative itself, was so diminished that he might be persuaded of the reality of even the most laughable rumor; and it was fortunate, he told himself, that the priests of his mission-dwelling days, men for whom charity was more drug than virtue, weren't around, or else he would be down on his knees, howling to Jesus, while one of them, maybe the Jesuit with the hair plugs in Seattle, Father Brad, what an asshole!, clasped his hands and beamed at him fatuously.... Informed by all this, then, Wilander returned to his maps, attacking his cartographer's problem with fresh inspiration and renewed zeal, making corrections, refining his vision of a nameless country populated by transparent badgers and invisible birds and gigantic flying worms, adding detail to a map of the city encircling the lagoon (the buildings inland low and undistinguished, like housing developments; those nearer the water arranged in complexes that radiated outward from the palatial structure on the peninsula), and also detailing the well-notched coastline beyond the city and a grouping of six islands that bore signs of habitation, laboring long into the night, damping his fears with work, quelling his rational concerns, forgetting everything.

* * *

    A chilly morning in late August when frost sheathed the railings and mist clothed the firs in ghostly rags at dawn, thickening to a dense fog as the day wore on, hiding the world, the sun growing no brighter than a weak pewter glare, and Wilander lay beneath the linden tree, drowsing, clad in T-shirt and boxers, wrapped in a blanket, now and again opening an eye to squint at the grayish-white grainy stuff into which the deck disappeared, then falling back asleep, having a trifling dream or two; and, when he woke to see a dark shape in the mist, a phantom shape, he refused to believe in it and shut his eyes, but when he looked in that same direction a minute later, it was still there, closer, darker, more fearsome, undeniably real, and he sat up, clutching his blanket, shouted, *Hey! Hey!* and stumbled to his feet, overbalanced, caught himself on the railing, and so was standing in a half-crouch among the linden boughs, gaping, his heart slamming, as Terry Alpin hove into view wearing his official uniform, black leather jacket, jeans, T-shirt, holding a cigarette that released a thread of smoke, making it seem as if that slim white tube had once contained all the mist and was down to its last trickle.

Wilander straightened and adjusted his blanket, striving for dignity, and pushed aside one of the boughs to give himself a more complete view of Terry. Where the hell did you come from?

—Boat. Terry glanced off along the deck. Damn! It must be eight, nine years since I been out here.

—Boat, said Wilander dully.

—My dad's launch. Terry gestured at the door of the officers' mess. I can get down to the engine room that way, right?

—What do you want down there?

—I'm gonna see if I can find my Uncle Frank's initials. It's where he used to sleep.

—Your uncle was part of the crew?

—Naw, man. When *Viator* ran aground, when people were coming out to rip shit off, Frank, he thought it was pretty cool, this big-ass ship in the middle of the trees. Then him and his wife had problems, so he says, Fuck, I'm moving to *Viator*. He didn't stay long. Maybe a month. He said it was making him sick.

—Sick...like how?

—Sick in the head, dude. He was having fucked-up

dreams and shit. Hey, your bathroom work? That's one thing really messed up Frank. Having to walk through the hold, so he could go outside and piss. It was so dark down there, it freaked him out.

—Everything works, Wilander said, muzzily trying to frame a follow-up question.

Terry tore off one of the linden leaves and examined it. Weird. These should've started to turn. Couple, three weeks, we'll be into winter pretty much.

—Yeah, well. We're having kind of a fifth season out here. Lots of weird stuff. Feeling a chill, Wilander caught the blanket more tightly about his throat. What do you want?

—What do *I* want? Not to be here, man. I got shit to take care of. Arlene wanted to find you, so I rode her out.

—Arlene's here?

—Yep. Terry flipped his cigarette over the railing.

The idea that Arlene had boarded the ship both dismayed and pleased Wilander, and for a second or two he was unable to react. Where is she? he asked.

—Trying to find you, dude. You might want to clean up before she sees you. You look like you been sleeping with the dogs.

Wilander hesitated, uncertain in which direction to move—his cabin, for a clean-up, or should he try to find her now? The latter, he decided; otherwise she might encounter one of the crew and he did not trust their reactions.

—'Course, said Terry, I guess she's seen you looking funky before. So what the hell.

—Is she below decks?

—I think, yeah.

Wilander started away, paused and said, If you run into anyone else, tell them you have my permission to be on board.

—Why? You think your buddies are gonna throw me over the side? Terry removed a second cigarette, previously hidden by his long hair, from behind his ear. I been coming here since I was a kid. I don't need nobody's permission.

One of the metal-throated birds took that moment to cry out and Terry, with a puzzled expression, turned to look for the source of the sound.

—The place may have changed, Wilander said. You never know what you might need.

He hurried along the passageway of the officer's deck, thinking Arlene might be down at the opposite end, by the galley and the stairs leading to the engine room, but as he passed the mess he saw her standing beside the dining table. She was wearing a red-and-black plaid wool jacket and jeans, her hair tied back, and she was peering at his maps, which were scattered about on table, chairs, and floor. The light from the ports seemed ancient light, the light of centuries past, the pearly gray glow that Vermeer used to cast a glum benediction upon the subjects of certain portraits—it limned her figure and lent her skin a low polish, as of marble. 'Morning, he said, and she flicked a glance his way, the sort of look you'd give an incompetent waiter before turning your eyes away and asking for the check in a surly voice. She indicated the maps and

VIATOR

asked, This is why you needed the sketchpads?

—It's just something to pass the time.

—You felt a need to pass the time? The tedium was that great? Being with me is so boring, you prefer...what? She swatted at the maps, knocking several to the floor, anger breaking through her neutral pose. What's this all about?

—Maps. Wilander went a few steps into the room. How can you say I'm bored with you?

She put a forefinger to her chin, making a show of pondering the question. Let's see. Not hearing from you for three days, that was my first clue.

—It hasn't been three days!

—Does time pass more slowly? How long do you think it's been?

Wilander couldn't come up with a number, but realized it might have been longer than he thought. It's been three days? Really?

Arlene spat out a disgusted noise and stared down at the table once again. Maps of what? she asked.

—I'm sorry. I don't understand how it happened. I must...I don't know. Maybe....

—Maps of what? She slapped the table with her palm and shrilled at him. What? What is this?

Again, Wilander was so disconcerted. he could only offer a stammering reply. I told you, it's nothing, just...just a....

—They have something to do with *Viator*, don't they? She idled along the table, inspecting more of the maps. You're crazy like the rest of them.

—It's not crazy. I'm not sure how to explain it, but....

—But I'm dying to hear your explanation! Are they, like, your rust? Your broken glass?

—There's no use getting angry.

—I'm not angry. Not anymore.

—Yeah, I can tell.

—Okay, I'm angry. Three days without a word, I was....

—We didn't sign any papers, said Wilander resentfully.

In Arlene's stare, in the configuration of fine lines around her eyes and at the corners of her mouth, he saw scorn directed at him and also at herself, the self-ridicule of a woman who had committed an act of folly, one she had committed many times before and had sworn never to repeat.

—I was worried, she said. I thought you might be sick. I didn't realize you had such important work to do. She took a less aggressive swat at the maps. You're damn right, I'm angry. And I'm sad. She snatched up a sheet of sketch paper and thrust it at him. Go ahead. Explain it to me.

—So you can make fun of me? That's what you want?

—So I can understand what's wrong with you. Her voice broke and she struggled to control her features. I know there's something wrong.

The tension between them softened and wavered, but when neither one moved to close the distance or to speak, Wilander sensed it hardening again, and their silence might have held if Terry hadn't entered the mess, coming up behind Wilander and asking Arlene how much longer she intended to stay, then, on spotting the maps, brushing past him to have a look and saying, What's all this shit? And

Wilander, forced by Terry's interruption to adopt some stance, to break the tension, called their attention to the wall and asked if they saw the landscape thereon. He pointed out firs, hills, the city, the lagoon, the coastline, the islands, feeling foolish as he did, certain that he was confirming Arlene's characterization of his behavior, but at the same time feeling defiant, secure in what he believed, as if her challenge had confirmed something in him, the knowledge that he was not crazy, and given a reliable value to all the things he half-believed about *Viator*—they were true; perhaps not wholly accurate, but true. And they were significant. He was onto something here. Do you see it? he asked, and Arlene admitted, It's there, yeah. Terry fiddled with his lighter, clicking it open and shut, appearing disinterested. That's what the maps are of, Wilander said. You can see different views of the same place on the other walls.

Arlene said, They're becoming visible...the pictures? They weren't always there?

—That's right.

She fingered the edge of one map, studying it. Let's say that's true....

—I can show you! Every wall—almost all of them—has an image of the same exact place. It can't be coincidence.

—Fine. But I don't have time for a tour, so let's say it's true. Arms folded, she came to stand facing him, a foot away. That's the reason you're staying here?

Wilander examined the question for traps, found none, and decided not to lie. Sometimes I don't want to stay, but...yes.

—You're staying so you can make maps of a place you claim the ship is showing you. Do you see anything wrong with that?

—I'm not crazy.

—I'm not saying you are! I'm accepting that what you say is true. It's a supernatural event. Pictures are materializing on the walls of the ship and you're going to stay on board and make maps from them. That doesn't scare you? It doesn't cause you to think the situation might be unhealthy? Dangerous? That you might be safer elsewhere? Somewhere the walls aren't turning into pictures?

—I think, Wilander said cautiously, I need to be here for now.

She put a hand to her brow and let out a breath. How long do you figure *for now* is?

—Arlene. Wilander reached out to touch her shoulder, but she pulled away. He glanced at Terry and said, Why don't you give us some space?

—No, don't! Arlene signaled Terry to keep still. I'm almost done.

—I'll go back to town with you, Wilander said.

—Not tonight, you won't! You need to stay here, you need to give careful thought to what you're doing.

—What does that mean?

—It means I want you to decide! Take a few days if you want. Take a week. But decide. I can't handle this anymore. I shouldn't have to.

Terry sidled toward the passageway. I'll be on deck.

—It'd be nice if you called, Arlene said to Wilander. You know, to tell me what you've decided? But either way, if I don't hear soon, my door will be closed. I won't live like this.

—Live like what? I told you I'd leave after the first snowfall. I thought we agreed to that.

—I don't believe you. I don't believe you believe it yourself. Whatever's going on with you, with the ship, it's not good. You're not in control.

—Look, I know this has been tough, and I wish things were different. I wish we'd met at a more propitious time. He took her hand, applied a light pressure, and though she did not return his pressure, she allowed his fingers to mingle with hers. But all this...all coming at once. You, the job, *Viator*. It's been....

—I don't want to hear about your problems anymore! She stepped around him and went to stand in the doorway. I worry about what's happening to you. I worry all the time! But I've lived long enough, I've learned I can't save anybody by hovering over them while they work out their problems. They take it for license; they convince themselves that on some level I must enjoy watching and waiting, or that I can tolerate it...or something! I'm going to worry about myself from now on. And you have to worry about yourself. Or not. That's up to you. Do you understand?

Wilander couldn't think what to say. Words occurred to him, too many words, words attached to feelings that, if not contrary to one another, seemed unrelated, as if he were feeling everything at once—anger, regret, love, several varieties of fear, even a perverse satisfaction at having so splendidly and so relentlessly mishandled the relationship.

She asked again if he understood, demanding an answer, and he said, I think I've got it. Yeah.

She looked to be gathering herself, preparing, he thought, a goodbye; then, suddenly alert, she said, Oh! I have some news. It's really the reason I came. I wasn't going to, but I learned something you should know, and my phone was acting up. I did a search on the Internet for your employer.

—Lunde?

—There wasn't much information. He's spoken at a few conferences on unemployment. Things like that. But here's the part that'll interest you. Guess who *Viator*'s captain was when she ran aground?

Wilander gawked at her.

—Jochanan Lunde. Your benefactor. Her eyes flashed to his face, then away, as if she were assessing the effect of this revelation, yet didn't want him to catch the malicious expression that briefly surfaced, a malice he had sparked in her, that had remade an intended kindness into an intent to wound and confuse him, as she had been wounded and confused. What do you make of that? she asked, her tone too bright to communicate concern. Maybe he doesn't have your welfare at heart after all.

Once she had gone, Wilander tried to balance the implications of Lunde's duplicity with his own appreciation of *Viator*, and, finding no logic to diminish the sinister light in which Arlene's news cast Lunde's motives, he hurried to his cabin, threw on some clothes and headed for the stern, hoping to beg a ride into town with Terry. Given what he now knew, to spend another night on board would be foolhardy. Whatever Lunde had in mind, it had nothing to do with salvage (apparent from the start) and still less to do with charity (something now apparent), and Wilander could only believe that he and the others were being manipulated along some extraordinary and, almost assuredly, perilous course, like lab rats in a run. Upon reaching the stern, he called out to Arlene, unable to locate her in the fog, and, receiving no response, he shinnied down the rope that he had tied to the railing. As he hung above the shingle, he heard a motor cough, stutter, and catch. Arlene! he shouted, and quickened his descent. Trotting along the margin of the shore, he shouted again. He slipped on the wet pebbles, his right foot raising a splash, and spotted a dark shape gliding off, barely identifiable as two figures in a boat, there for an instant, then not there, the trebly grind of the motor growing muffled, dwindling and dwindling, soon outvoiced by the lapping tide. He dropped into a squat, oppressed, rendered energy-less by a feeling of loss and isolation. As soon as the weather eased, he told himself, he would walk into town. Not at night, though. He didn't trust the forest at night. A damp west wind gusted, thickening the briny smell, giving things a stir, the boughs, wavelets, seaweed, and stirring as well the becalmed waters of his thoughts. He wished he had made himself clearer to Arlene from the inception of the affair; instead of simply saying that he wasn't solid, leading her to think that his recovery was the main issue, a matter of getting settled, getting straight in his head, he should have said that he wasn't strong enough to take on her entire life. That's what she was looking for, someone who would embrace her hopes and dreams, her beliefs, someone who would cherish those things even if he couldn't share them, who would consider them in every situation. He should have emphasized the fact that he wanted to be that person, but she had to be patient, because—as he'd told her—it was disorienting to have so much life after years of having none, and it was going to take some time before he understood how much was left of him. How much strength. How much capacity for love. How much honesty. He should have done all that and more. The wind gusted harder, the fog eddied, and the shapes of the firs at the south end of the shingle sharpened into the dark green ghosts of trees. No sound came, except for wind and the slurp of the tide. Limbo, he thought. Purgatory. Neither heaven nor hell, yet judged closer to hell for the absence of heaven. At his feet, black water edged with a lacy froth filmed among the pebbles, creeping to his toes, floating up twigs and dried needles. He clenched a pebble in his fist; its cold solidity steadied him and he imagined that if he continued to hold it, it would infect his flesh, turning him to stone, and years hence he would be found squatting on the shore, a small boulder weathered by magical storms (so it would be said) into a rude approximation of a man worshipped by the elder Inupiats, those who had not yet learned to discredit the miraculous nature of existence—they would drape him with kelp necklaces, they would paint images of the sea upon his eyes, they would dress him in bark and feathers, leave him food and drink, give him names, and when the last of them were dead, then he, too, would die, a neglible transition, since even prior to his transformation, his life had been a flicker of self-awareness, nothing more. Unaccountably weary, his joints cracking, he stood and sidearmed the pebble across the water, listening for the plop, and then started back to the ship. The hull loomed overhead. It appeared larger than he recalled, as if some gross internal disorder had caused it to bloat while he was distracted. With its abraded belly, listing a few degrees to port, centering the ragged frame of the forest, veiled in drifts of mystic gray, the convulsed screws and the bolt-stitched plates adding a brutal Frankensteinian touch, *Viator* no longer posed a vast metal incongruity, a surreal element of the landscape, but had acquired the monstrous, mythical aspect of a mighty life stranded, like an old whale confounded by pollution and driven to beach itself, yet still vital, generating by its restive vitality the pulse of the silence that engulfed the place; and, though Wilander approached the ship fearfully, his fear was not a shriveling fear, a fear of the unknown, but the anxiety of someone who had happened upon a moribund giant and was worried it might lash out in its pain and desperation, and inadvertently crush him. Four figures materialized at the rail above, occulted by the fog, and he halted his approach. He couldn't tell one from the other, but when three of them withdrew, he assumed that the sole remaining figure, its outlines blurring and sharpening with the alternations of the fog, was Mortensen. Not a word passed between them, but some unspoken message may have been exchanged, some frail accord summoned, for Wilander, inspired by a sympathy more poignant than the sympathetic reaction naturally incurred by two strangers sharing a solitude, lifted his hand in salute. The fog looked to be weaving a cocoon about Mortensen. returning him to the cloudy dimension where he hermited. Within seconds, he was hidden from view. Wilander waited for a reply, his neck craned, but the figure never reemerged.

Seven

"...Cape Lorraine and environs..."

Wilander lost track of the fog's duration (days, certainly) because he wanted to lose track, to muffle his fears, to blunt his every understanding, and, toward this end, channeled his energies into the creation of maps: terrain maps of the hills that built inland from the coastal city; a street map of the southernmost quarter of the city; maps of the island grouping, rudimentary except for that of the largest island, shaped like a tail-less stingray and supporting a town on its seaward end; maps of the coastline to the north, recently revealed by images emerged from the walls of the bridge; maps roughed out in pencil and, once he was sure of their accuracy, painstakingly redrawn in ink and shaded with pastels, as he once had done for extra credit in his fourth grade geography class, attempting to curry favor with Mrs. Louise Gatch—a gaunt, fiftyish, deathshead Marine colonel trapped in a teacher's body, she still patrolled the halls of Wilander's memory, ready to pounce at the slightest sign of smudged lines or bad penmanship. He strayed from his station in the officers' mess to cook and piss and sleep, but for no other reason, pausing often to phone Arlene, who was probably screening her calls and refusing to pick up; however, he could not bring himself to phone Lunde—he dreaded what the old man might say and decided to wait until he was well away from *Viator*, when the information, whatever it might be, would have no power to menace him. Soon the desire to talk with Lunde left him and the maps came to occupy him to the exclusion of all else and he began to add details that were not shown on the walls, making these additions surehandedly, swiftly, as if he were remembering things about the city and the shore, and, as this apparent familiarity deepened, he took to naming portions of his imagined landscape. The names bubbled forth from the depths of his mind, solitary words and random syllables, sounds that aligned with other sounds: Sirkasso Beach, a sandy crescent along the inner edge of the lagoon; Cotaliri Bay, a notch in the coastline to the south; Mutikelio, one of the islands, and the islands themselves, the group he named the Six Tears, a reference to the legend that, millennia ago, tears had spilled from the eyes of a giant as he died and these were the seeds about which the islands had grown, whereas his bones had petrified and now constituted a section of the coast, the waters of the lagoon being enclosed by an orbital socket, and it was claimed that threads of protein from the giant's humor still drifted at the bottom of the lagoon and swimmers there were thus prone to see things that he had seen in life, relic visions of the barbarous world in which he had thrived, and occasionally some feature of those visions would become real, a predatory fish or a moasaur or an undersea castle, an architectural fantasy of curving pink towers, dozens of towers, a veritable anemone among castles, to which an expedition had been dispatched, all of whose members vanished when the castle rippled and faded and washed from sight. Further scraps of lore attached themselves to every name Wilander applied to the maps, and before long he recognized that he was creating not merely a series of maps, but the traditions and natural history of the area mapped, a section of coast known as the Iron Shore due to the color of the rocks that guarded its length, its forests populated by wiccara (the sluggish, wonderfully camouflaged ground animals) and qwazil (the always hidden metal-throated birds); and, among other elusive creatures, the whistlers, a shy, slender, physically beautiful subhuman folk with whom it was forbidden to mate, although such liasions were commonplace due to the pheromone-laced perfume they could release at will, and were especially common during the winters, when famine drove the whistlers into the outskirts of the city, searching for food (the remainder of the time they subsisted by hunting small animals, killing them with piercing whistles pitched too high for the human ear to detect); and from the skies the wormlike fliers of Wilander's dreams would swoop down to terrify the city, yet never attacking, never damaging life or property, as if they had an intellectual interest in the place and were driven to check on it on a regular basis. Cape Lorraine was the city's name, a name deriving from the fact that the original settlement had been established on the peninsula that formed the outer edge of the lagoon, and when Wilander arrived at that name, he was intrigued by its commonality in contrast to the rest and explored his memory, trying to recall if there might have been a significant Lorraine in his past, but the only Lorraine he could recall was Lorraine Scheib, a friend of a friend during his college years, an aggressively plain lesbian girl who wore overalls and wrote violent anti-male poetry, and it seemed this might be an indicator that he was not inventing the names, he was remembering them, that as *Viator* sailed closer to the Iron Shore, moving in its mysterious fashion, coursing along a metaphysical northwest passage, he—borne along with it—was receiving increasingly elaborate impressions of their destination, just as a sailor peering from the bow of a landward-bearing ship would receive impressions of the coast, its scents, its colors, its configuration. Though not a new thought, it was newly credible, and the possibility that he was somehow seeing what lay ahead for them made him afraid. He set aside the maps for a night and sat at the table wrestling with the problem of whether to call Lunde, but couldn't keep his focus and began drowsily leafing through his memories of Arlene until one stuck in his head: watching her put on her bra, as she stood naked by the bathroom door, with lemony dawn light behind her, bending at the waist so as to let her breasts fall into a shape that would more readily conform to the cups, a pose an artist might choose for its intimacy, its graceful female specificity, the nearly perfect horizontal of her back, her legs positioned as if she were a ballerina bowing into a curtsey, responding to imagined applause, alone in an empty theater where she one day hoped to triumph. He couldn't fathom why the memory seemed sad; he remembered that morning well, a good morning, a happy morning, and he supposed that remembrance itself was by nature sad, or perhaps women's relation to their breasts was intrinsically sad, something about their simultaneous gift and limitation, how they served as emblems of both ripeness and inadequacy.... Something. Lonely for her, he dug out his phone and called. To his surprise, she answered on the fourth ring.

—Please don't hang up, he said.
—Thomas. Her voice was tired. What do you want?
—Just to talk.
—I don't think that's a good idea.
—If you didn't want to talk, why'd you answer?
—I was falling asleep—I forgot to look at the caller ID.
—What time is it?
—After eleven sometime.
—Sorry.

She made a diffident noise and he said, You wouldn't have answered if you saw it was me?

—Is this what you want to talk about? About whether or not I want to talk?
—No.

He would have liked to tell her about Cape Lorraine, the Iron Shore, but it wasn't the kind of thing he could explain over the phone; he'd have to sit her down face-to-face and persuade her to listen to everything, to react unemotionally. He thought to ask how she was doing, canceled that because she would probably respond with irony, and finally said, I miss you, and added hurriedly, I realize that's my fault, but it's true nonetheless.

She was silent, then an indrawn breath, signaling that

she had started to speak; then another brief silence. Would it make you happy if I said I missed you? she asked.

—No, it wouldn't make me happy. Arlene, I....

—Why did you call? What do we have to talk about? Should I tell you the latest gossip? I got in the plasma TV Gary ordered for the bar. Is that what you're after?

—If it works for you.... Yeah. I'd settle for it.

Despairingly, she said, God! Why did you call?

—The truth? I was remembering watching you get dressed one morning. I got lonely.

He heard her television switch on, a voice blaring.

—It's been ten days, she said.

That seemed too big a number, but he couldn't prove it. I'm past the deadline, huh?

—That wasn't my point. I was remarking that it's taken you ten days to get lonely.

—Not really. It didn't take ten minutes.

—All right. It's taken you ten days to feel lonely enough to call.

—I didn't mean it to go ten days.

—I know. You got busy. With your maps. Time just flew by!

Visible in the deck lights, a curl of fog squirmed against the glass of the port; over the phone, he heard what might have been a comedian telling jokes, an audience laughing. If I was to come into town tonight, he said, how would that be?

—I'm not going to answer that. It's not a real question. You're not coming in tonight. You won't come in tomorrow. Eventually, I suppose, you'll drag yourself into town, but I'm not expecting you anytime soon.

Her tone, in the span of those five sentences, had gone from embittered to angry, and he tried to mollify her, but she wouldn't allow it, she kept talking over him, and at last she yelled, Shut up! Okay? Don't say anything for a minute! Please! They had always been at cross-purposes, he realized. Always off by at least a degree or two, never quite equal in commitment or desire, in the direction they were seeking to push the relationship, always making slight, off-center shifts that left them imperfectly aligned—even at the beginning, when Arlene had been seductive, he had feared a disappointment and suppressed his emotions. Most of that was his fault as well. He'd had responsibilities.

—After tonight, she said, calm now, I don't want you to call for a while.

—How long's a while?

—I'll tell you when I know.

He let four or five seconds drag past and was about to speak when she said, It's okay to call if there's an emergency. Or if it's about supplies. Then I'll put you on with Terry. But otherwise....

—I understand.

The recognition that she needed to be alone so she could kill off her feelings made him hate the world. He flung himself out of the chair and walked along the wall opposite, trailing his fingers over the Iron Coast, touching the Six Tears, six spots of rust in the lime sherbet sea, taking consolation from their strangeness, their valuable, validating strangeness, from all the strangeness of *Viator*. The immensity of the ship seemed to solidify around him, to grow suddenly palpable; he thought he could feel its shape and weight and dimensions particularly, the long, honeycombed half-cylinder of the hull wedged in place, as if the iron were a skin and he the nerve through which *Viator* transmitted its nightly report.

—Where are you? Arlene asked. In your room?

—Cape Lorraine and environs, he said, picking at a flake of paint on the edge of Mutikelio Island, wondering if he were to pull it loose, if the island did exist in the world next door, would that alter its geography?

—What?

—I'm in the mess.

After a pause she said, Did you call Lunde?

—I make my reports, but if you're asking did I bring up what you told me.... No, I didn't.

—Why not?

—I haven't got around to it. I'll call him again soon.

—Don't you want to know why he sent you here?

—I'm not sure him being *Viator*'s captain has anything to do with that. All it means is he knew about the ship.

—But why wouldn't he tell you he was captain?

—Why would he?

—He was your friend! Telling you he was captain of a ship that he was sending you to salvage, to live on...that would be natural for a friend. He'd tell you things only he knew. He might want you to report on how his cabin looked, or if you found where he carved his initials.

—Swedish men of his generation, they don't tend to be chatty about their pasts.

—Perhaps not. But this was such an important part of his life. Did I tell you...I can't remember. About him losing his license? His company was going to prosecute him. He must have gone through hell. What happened with *Viator* changed everything for him.

—All the more reason he wouldn't talk about it. He's probably ashamed. Maybe he was drunk. Maybe that's all that happened. He was drunk, he lost it and ruined his career.

He no longer heard the comedian and assumed that Arlene had gone into the living room and pictured her throwing magazines off the sofa and lying down, wearing her plaid flannel pajamas, the phone tucked between her shoulder and jaw; he went out onto the deck so he might feel closer to her, removing the barrier of iron, separated from her by darkness and trees alone.

—The maps, the other stuff you've talked about, Arlene said. Aren't you anxious to learn what he knows?

—I'm interested, but not anxious.

—You know, I don't understand this. Ever since I met you, you've been dying to know what Lunde had in mind, and now you're all blasé.... Like, whatever.

—I'm going to call him. All right? But it's not the most urgent thing on my mind.

—What could be more urgent? It's not like you're overtaxed out there.

He started to say, no, he wasn't overtaxed, not like her, he had no important inventory to take of spark plugs, tampons, Diet-Rite, string cheese (a favorite Inupiat treat), nothing so pressing as that, but he didn't want an argument, no more than was already in the air, and he said, I'll take care of it soon. I promise.

—We're past making promises. Do it or don't do it. It's not my concern anymore.

He walked along the deck, moving toward the bow, passing beyond range of the spill of light from the mess, keeping a hand on the rail to guide himself through the dark. We don't have to be enemies, do we? he asked. Even if you consider me worthless, an idiot, we can treat each other respectfully.

—For now, I have to be your enemy...a little.

He had the notion that the silence surrounding him was pouring out of the phone from Arlene's apartment, which was flooded with an endless supply. The damp and chill of the night worked beneath his skin. He considered asking what would happen between them if he came to her a week from now, a month, but realized that whatever answer she gave, it would somehow serve to harden a negative attitude. I guess I should let you go, he told her.

—Yeah, I've got to sleep. Another early morning tomorrow.

—Okay. Well.... Good night.

—Good night.

He had felt only intermittently connected with her during the call, sparks and flickers, the sputtering of a faulty connection, but after switching off the phone, he felt that a protective envelope had dissipated, the cold moving in to fill the vacuum, and he shoved his hands into his pockets, hunched his shoulders, leaning against the rail at the very peak of the bow (was there a word for that precise spot, the last firm footing behind the prow, some Latinate term, the perigolum, the spitaline, or maybe a vulgar British term dating from the days of the lash?) amid the spicy smell of the firs, peering off into the night, unable to make out a trunk, a bough, a fern, and then seeing shapes melt up from the darkness, amoeboid blotches of a shinier black than the air, shiny like patches of worn velvet, gliding and jittering across his field of vision, a whole zoo of them slipping about, and he thought that here in this forward position, at the edge of *Viator*, aloft from the world, he should have a perfect angle on things, a true perspective in every direction, even inward, unless such an angle was impossible and no matter what promontory you scaled, hoping to penetrate the incidental distractions that blinded you to your life, to understand its central circumstance, you discovered that you had no central circumstance, no fundamental issue, no rational pivot by which to steer—it was all distraction, all a flowing (according to Heraclitus, at least), a flux impossible to navigate, and you were borne along on unknowable currents and tides until you, the mad captain of your soul, ran yourself aground on the reef of a heap of white powder, a homeless shelter, an abandoned ship, an abandoned relationship...and sometimes that tactic worked out for the best, as it may have for Lunde, as it might have for Wilander if he'd had the good sense to strand himself on the shoal of the trading post and cultivate the illusion of a central circumstance with Arlene. It could work out yet. He would have to surrender himself to the principles of the relationship, principles they'd establish, but a week or a month from now, perhaps longer, he could walk into town and, after a probationary period, after hurt feelings had been soothed, she would take him back. He hated the confidence that knowing this gave him; it tempted him to believe she loved him more than he loved her, and he refused to believe that. Despite mis-alignments, tentativeness, and ungainly steps (and how else could a dance like theirs have proceeded, two people so unused to each other, so variant in their experience, going from strangers to lovers in the space of a few weeks, a few walks, a few conversations, very similar to how things had developed between him and Bliss Zouski, except the situation had been reversed, she'd been the one drawn by some mysterious force to withdraw from the affair, money or security, some more reasonable incarnation of *Viator*, some powerful edifice or mass of philosophical iron that magnetized her will, pulling her toward a false north), he believed they were equal in their mutual attraction and, once past this blunder, once he ridded himself of his fixation with the ship, once he felt solid.... This thought, a trial balloon floated, an attempt at bravado, didn't have enough lift to complete itself, because he was no longer sure he had the will to take that walk. *Viator*'s hold had tightened on him; in that, he was no different from Arnsparger or Nygaard or Halmus. Mortensen, now.... Perhaps Mortensen was different, or perhaps he was simply farther along the path. Wilander leaned forward over the prow, imagining himself to be the ship's tiny figurehead, wishing that he felt as unassailable as a figurehead. As stoic. His vision had adjusted and he could see intimations of trees, of a limb half-snapped away from its trunk, drooping in front of *Viator*, and he had an apprehension of the great entanglement and complexity in which he lived, the vines and toadstools, the rotting logs and mattes of compressed, decaying branches, the beds of salvia carpeting the earth, the vivid productions of mold and moss, the chains of his life, verdant and virtual. Everything was still. Then a noise broke from the depths of the forest, a faint but distinct groaning. Not a sound generated by flesh and bone—it was unmistakably the groan of metal under stress. Simultaneously, in the distance, farther away than he had thought it possible to see in a straight line, given the obstructions of hills and trees, a corruscant white light flared and shrank, flared again, like the sputter of a welder's torch. The groaning escalated into a shriek; the light fluctuated wildly, growing so bright, it threw into silhouette the shapes of tangled coils and loops that looked to be close by the radiant source. Vines? Wire? They were gone before Wilander could make a more informed guess. The light fizzled, winked out; the groaning lapsed; a breath of warm air touched his face, carrying a richly bitter scent and then something sweet, almost a chocolate smell, a smell such as might be released from a barista's cart. The stillness of the forest had been abolished. Metal-throated qwazil lamented on high. From the hill to starboard came a concentrated rustling, as of small animals stampeding through the underbrush. Wilander squeezed the rail, all his muscles tight, intent upon these sounds and other, less familiar cries: a repeated passage of seven rapid, hollow notes, reminiscent of notes on a glockenspiel; a shrill attenuated quavering, like the whine of an open frequency; a soft mammalian chuffing. He did not seek to rationalize what he saw and smelled and heard, nor did he stand long at the rail. The cold began to bother him. He turned from the prow and walked toward the yellow glare chuting from the door of the officer's mess and, as he stepped inside, the qwazil that haunted the linden gave its cry, louder than usual, its articulations plainer, as if it had roosted lower in the tree, and what had previously come to Wilander's ear as sorrowful now seemed to illustrate a more complicated quality, a weary yet joyful relief like that expressed by a lookout, aloft for days, who—having sighted a dark green line on the horizon or a seagull riding a landward current—called down to his mates that their long voyage was nearly done.

Eight

"....What the fuck's wrong with you..."

The morning following the first snowfall, a light snow that sugared the tops of the fir boughs and the boulders along the shore and left the decks slick, Wilander, sitting in the officers' mess, phoned Jochanan Lunde to make his report, and when the old man asked if anything out of the ordinary had occurred, Wilander related the tale of his months aboard *Viator*, omitting nothing, inflecting each incident with a kind of venomous relish (You want out of the ordinary? Take a bite of this!) that, he thought, might have been brought on by his long repression of it—he told Lunde about the recurring dreams, the ropy flying creatures that dominated them, about Mortensen's apocryphal admonitions, about the maps that appeared on the walls, about the wiccara and the qwazil, about the blazing lights and the groans that issued from the heart of the forest (a phenomenon repeated on three occasions thusfar), and he further related his thoughts and feelings about these matters, his ongoing invention of a history and ecology to suit Cape Lorraine and the Iron Shore, his *idée fixe* that *Viator*'s journey might not have not ended. And after the old man failed to offer an immediate response, other than to mutter a curse in Swedish, not a wicked curse, but a profane word used in astonishment, Wilander asked Lunde to explain why he had sent them to live onboard the ship, saying that he refused to believe that they were doing preliminary work for a salvage operation.

Lunde kept silent a few seconds longer and then said, I don't wish to talk about this. Perhaps we can touch on it next time.

—Why not now?

—I have business to attend. But keep me informed, will you? It might be helpful for you to call more frequently. Every few days or so. Now...are you set with supplies?

—We have food and water for three months. We could stand to lay in some more gas for the generator. It'll take longer to order once winter's here.

—Very well. Order it. And call me. Call me Friday. From now on why don't you call every Friday as well as Mondays?

At this juncture, Wilander, after months of worrying that the old man might become angry and terminate them, caught something in Lunde's voice, an undercurrent of excitement breaking through his stern manner, that made him realize that he, not his employer, held the upper hand. You're not hearing me, he said. I want to know what's going on.

—I beg your pardon?

—With *Viator*. I want to know what's happening to us.

—You're not making sense. How can I help you with that? I'm not there with you.

—Yeah, you've said that before. But you were *Viator*'s captain. You were aboard when she ran aground. That's what I want to hear about.

—How did you learn this? Lunde asked.

—Don't worry about it. Just tell me what went on.

Flustered, Lunde said, It's not in my interests to discuss the subject. I'm not permitted to, uh…. There are legal issues, you see. I'm not….

—Let me be clear. If you won't talk to me, I'll pull the crew off the ship.

Lunde fell silent again and, afraid that his bluff would be called, because he wasn't certain that he could pull himself off the ship, let alone the others, or that he could even find them all, because it had been a week since he'd seen Mortensen and several days since he'd seen Halmus, Wilander decided that the wisest course was to raise his own bluff and said, I'll pull them off today. I may not be able to move Nygaard. And Mortensen may resist. But neither of those guys is capable of making reports. Nygaard's a borderline idiot and Mortensen's turned into John the fucking Baptist. And that's what this is about, isn't it? The reports? You need somebody to tell you what's going on. There's something about *Viator* you want to know. You must be desperate to know it. Why else spend so much money and effort to send us here?

—I can't tell you anything, Lunde said weakly. You've already gone past….

Wilander waited for him to continue; finally, to prompt him, he asked, Past what?

—Maybe I know enough. Lunde's breath came ragged.

Maybe it's time to end this.

—If you think you know anything, Wilander said, I want to hear about it.

Lunde chuckled. I know I'm not just a crazy old man. That's more than I expected.

Wilander was dismayed by the chuckle—it implied that Lunde was looking from a remote, whimsical perspective upon a situation that he, Wilander, found deadly serious and far from remote. Do you want me to pull the crew? he asked. Or are you going to explain things to me?

—You may be disappointed with what I have to say. You've told me far more than I can tell you. But...why not? Hang on. I need to speak with my secretary. Muffled voices; papers rustling; a woman's laugh. All right. I'm back.

—I'm waiting.

—I was with *Viator* less than a year, Lunde said after a substantial pause. The company had promised me a new tanker, but there was a labor dispute. The tanker's construction was delayed. They gave me *Viator* as a temporary command. At the time she serviced a route between Yokahama and Magadan in Siberia...and on occasion down to Vladivostok. She was seaworthy, but in constant need of refitting and not long after I came aboard they decided to scrap her. The crew was Russian, mostly. They disembarked at Magadan, and five of us, five officers, a skeleton crew, were ordered to take her to Panama, where she would be broken. We were a few days....

—*Five* officers? Were they of Scandanavian blood, like the five of us?

—They were Swedish, Lunde said. The company's Swedish. The majority of officers are Swedish.

—What in God's name are you up to?

—You asked to hear my story. Now let me tell it. I'll explain as much as I'm able. Lunde made the sort of mild complaint that old men tend to make when they shift in their chairs and then went on: A few days out into the Bering Sea, we encountered a storm. It was nothing special. The sort of blow one expects in those latitudes. But we had no weight. Our cargo consisted of two small crates. Gifts from a company official to friends in Panama. That was all. The sea tossed us about as if *Viator* were a rowboat. On one occasion we nearly capsized. Then the engines failed, and it was a miracle we stayed afloat. If the winds had lasted an hour or two longer, I doubt we could have survived. Ulghren, my engineer, did an inspection. He told me that with two or three days, he could have the engines running. I consulted with my superiors, they consulted with theirs. It was decided that we would make repairs and continue our voyage south. Should another emergency arise, they would send rescue. Despite Ulghren's estimate, the repairs took more than a week. Eleven days, to be exact. He found it necessary to fabricate parts. The weather was holding. There seemed no cause for alarm. But during that time, things changed.

Lunde coughed and had difficulty in clearing his throat. This happened so long ago, he said. It's difficult to know how memory has transformed events. As I recall, the change was seamless. There were no moments of recognition when I said to myself, Aha! This is what's going on. It all happened so quickly, much more quickly than it's happened with you. Yet it was gradual. I noticed the changes, of course. The shifts in behavior, the differences in the way I thought. They seemed odd, these things. Odd enough to comment upon, but not anything I needed to be concerned about. Initially the men became secretive. I became secretive. And I began to have dreams. This is where our stories have the closest correspondence. My dreams were very like yours, except the flying things...I saw them as well, but they made me think of microscopic life. Like the creatures I observed under a microscope when I was a student.

—I recall thinking that myself, Wilander said. It was how they moved. It looked sometimes as if they were swimming, not flying.

—Swimmers, yes. That's how I perceived them. But the most compelling change was the sense I had—the sense we all had—of a subtle presence. I suspected that something had come to us during the storm. Nothing so ordinary as a ghost. Something not so easily describable. At times this feeling rose to the level of a *frisson*, but for the most part it was just something I was aware of, something disturbing in the back of my mind. Like a word you're seeking, one you can't quite put a finger on. Ulghren claimed the presence was *Viator*. *Viator* was alive, he claimed. Spekke and Ottendahl, my first and second mates, sided with him. Since they'd been assisting with repairs, I assumed Ulghren had influenced their opinions. And Kameus....

—You said you were secretive, all of you—yet you discussed what was happening?

—We had sailed together for almost a year. Kameus and I...Peter Kameus. He was my radio officer for almost eight years. So, yes, we discussed it. That was our training, our habit. But we discussed it superficially. We did not speak everything we thought. Not by a long shot. And as I was about to say, Kameus, my friend, my best friend...he deferred to me, he sided with me. But eventually I discovered that he had been paying lip service to my opinion.

—The point I'm making, Wilander said, is whatever the similarity between our stories, there's one major dissimilarity. You discussed what was happening among yourselves and we've done very little of that.

—It's as I said. We were a crew, conditioned to work together. If I could have recruited Swedish merchant officers to live aboard *Viator*, I would have done so. I hoped to recreate the conditions of the voyage as closely as possible. As things stood, I was forced to recruit five strangers. Men who had suffered psychological damage due to their homelessness and were conditioned to be distrustful. That you discuss the matter less than we did is hardly surprising. In retrospect, I think I may have been overly exacting. I think I could have put anyone aboard *Viator*. Their racial heritage, the number of men—I doubt these things were crucial.

Seething, Wilander said, A moment ago, when you said you weren't just a crazy old man...What the fuck's wrong with you? What gave you the right to use us?

—For twenty years I've been obsessed with what happened to *Viator*. I will admit to....

—I don't give a damn about your obsession. You had no right to make us part of an experiment.

—I won't deny it. But stop a moment! Think! Mortensen and Nygaard would not have seen the winter if I hadn't intervened in their lives. As for the rest of you, look at yourself. When you came into the office, you had nothing.

—No, no, no! Wilander said. Don't try to paint yourself as Saint Lunde. That's not going to fly.

—You had nothing, Lunde insisted. No prospects, no money, no friends. No hope. How much longer would you have lasted if I hadn't extended a hand? Another year? Two? Tell me how I've injured you.

—I don't know how. That's the problem. That's what we're talking about.

—Well, let's talk about it, then. I'll finish my story. That addresses your problem. After that we can discuss these other issues.

Wilander left his chair, too angry to speak, annoyed by Lunde's patronizing calm, and went to stand in the outer door of the mess. The day had grown bright and still, the air crisp, the firs were etched against the light. He stepped out onto the deck and walked toward the stern.

—Hello? Lunde said.

—Go ahead. Tell your story.

—Very well. Where was I?

—Repairing the engines. Discussing things.

—That's right. Yes. Lunde coughed again, a delicate cough this time, like punctuation. Our discussions were informal. If I was on the bridge with Spekke, say, the subject would come up. When I went to the engine room to check on the repairs, Ulghren and Ottendahl might mention it. Yet we never sat down to hash things out. We didn't talk at all when we were off-duty—off-duty, the men hid in their cabins. There was no more socializing. No drinking, no chatting. Nevertheless, the discussions, such as they were, grew heated. And it became apparent that our thoughts concerning *Viator* were developing along similar lines. The central thought, the one we agreed upon, was that *Viator* did not wish to die. What we failed to agree upon, however, was what should be done about this. On that matter, there was no consensus. Kameus, for instance, believed *Viator* had her own purposes and that we were interfering in them. An outsider would have thought us insane. But.... Well, you've experienced life aboard *Viator*. You understand how the insane can come to seem rational. Whenever I was alone, on the bridge or in my cabin, I plotted courses north and east from our position. I did not rely on the master charts; I made my own. Another officer would not have been able to read them—I coded their referents, wanting to keep them private. They expressed *Viator*'s will. She guided my hand as I drew. I knew her mind. I believed all this implicitly, although I tried to doubt it. It terrified me. If true, it was beyond my ability to understand. If false, I was crazy. And yet I also felt...blessed. I knew something remarkable was taking place, something that I could characterize generally, but couldn't put a precise name to.

—It's the same, Wilander said. There are differences, but the same thing is happening again.

He had stopped at the point on the rail where *Viator*'s stern emerged from the forest. Beyond, the sea stretched a glittering blue beneath a sky crowded with white clouds so huge and stately, they might have been migratory nations bursting with the purity of their founding ideals. The sight comforted him, not by its beauty, but by the fact that he seemed removed from it, as if it were something he was seeing through an airplane window.

—It's happened much more slowly for you, Lunde said. And perhaps the rest of the story speaks to that. By the time we finished the repairs, the relationships among the five of us had become strained. It remained my intention to continue south to Panama. Despite having faith in the charts I'd drawn, despite my belief that *Viator* had influenced their creation, I refused to acknowledge that *Viator*'s will was of more consequence than my career concerns. I wanted that new tanker. None of the others agreed, however, and tensions were high. One morning I was in my cabin, preparing for the day, when Kameus asked to speak with me. My memories of what occurred thereafter are unclear, but I imagine I turned my back on him. The next I recall, I was lying on the floor, my head throbbing. Kameus was standing above me, shouting something about *Viator*. I lost consciousness again and didn't wake until the mid-afternoon. Kameus had bound me and the sun was low before I managed to free myself. I took my sidearm and went searching for him. The ship was empty, the launch missing. They had abandoned me. I ran up to the radio room, intending to call for assistance, but Kameus had destroyed the receiver.

Lunde paused and Wilander heard a faint rapping that might have been the old man drumming his fingers on the desktop.

—I knew they must have made for Gambell on Saint Lawrence Island, Lunde said. It was less than a day from our position. But I have no idea how they managed to act together after being so thoroughly divided. No clue as to what informed their decision...or even if there was a decision. One of them may have taken control by force. At my hearing, they told the company I had gone mad and thrown them off the ship. How could I refute their story? They were four and I had run *Viator* aground. Those facts outweighed everything I said, anything I could have said. After I'd been stripped of my license, I telephoned Kameus and begged him to explain why they had done this, but he didn't trust the phone and he refused to meet with me. All he admitted was that he had been afraid. You know what I said to him? I said, You should have been alone aboard *Viator*. Then you could talk to me about fear. He hung up on me. My friend had abandoned me again and this second occasion was more painful, because he was no longer influenced by *Viator*. He was serving his own interests. Lunde let out a sigh. I'd never been afraid of the sea. I understood, of course, that it killed men and ships, but I had long since come to terms with that. Yet alone on *Viator*, I was afraid. The weather continued to hold. If I steered due east, I would harbor at Gambell in a matter of hours. I had no reason to fear, but I was panic-stricken. Partly this was due to the feeling that I was a flea riding atop an enormous metal beast. The ship's life seemed larger and more important than my own, and that of itself was frightening. But to this day I believe it was mainly *Viator*'s fear I felt. The product of her understanding that she would not survive another storm. Her desperation to reach land...though not just any landfall. She had a specific destination in view, one defined by my charts. With the engines half ahead—I didn't dare run them full—I steered north and east, bypassing Saint Lawrence and making for the Alaskan coast. Those next three days and nights, so much was going on in my mind, so many strange thoughts...of that time I can only clearly recall that I was afraid. I didn't sleep, I ate little. I trembled before the prospect of death, living in a fearful delirium, surrounded by my enemy, the sea. Until the very end. Until I saw that green haven north of Kaliaska. Then I was deliriously happy. It was early morning, mist everywhere, but I knew where to aim the bow. I lashed myself to the pilot's chair and ran the engines full ahead. To starboard, a fishing boat emerged from the mist, bearing straight for midships. There was a moment when my heart was in my throat and I feared we would be rammed, thrown off-course. But whoever was manning the fisherman's wheel avoided a collision. Watching the shingle widen ahead, I grinned as if I'd won some great contest and had no thought that I was about to destroy my career. The hull grating across the sand sounded like the bottom was being ripped out. If I hadn't secured myself to the chair, I would have been flung about and likely killed. And then the trees came up. *Viator* slewed and veered to port. I thought we would go over, but the boulders on either side kept us on an even keel. The noise.... It might have been the end of the world. Groans, shrieks, concussions. A wall of boughs loomed close. I ducked my head as the windows exploded inward. We kept on plowing forward, smashing deep into the forest, chewing up towering firs as if they were papier-mâché. And at last *Viator* was still. There were settling noises, and then silence.

Lunde made a clicking with his tongue, a vocal gesture that seemed to signal regret. I was dazed, he said. Dazed and groggy from shock, from lack of sleep, from stress. I sat staring out the glassless windows at the misted peace of the firs and was overcome by a feeling of calmness and security...though not of completion. I had no sense of finality. There was much more to do, I thought. What had gone before was just the beginning. I untied myself and made my way out onto the deck, going on unsteady legs toward the stern, intending to inspect the damage. The fisherman had followed us in, anchoring so close to shore, I could read its name and port of origin painted on a white tire that hung from its side: the Fat Allie out of Mayorkiq. They put forth a small boat bearing half-a-dozen men— Inupiat, judging by their complexions. They jumped out into the shallows and scrambled up the shingle. Some, I saw, carried rifles. Had I witnessed a ship run aground in a similar fashion, I would not have investigated without benefit of arms. Who knows what one might find onboard? But I assumed these men were bent on thievery and capable of worse. I hid in a storage locker off the bridge until I could no longer hear shouts and movement. Then I sneaked into the stern and watched them load their boat with tools, the big microwave from the galley, the crates consigned to Panama. Later I discovered they had stolen personal items from my cabin. And they were only the first vultures. Before the Fat Allie could get underway, townspeople began arriving in outboards and on foot through the forest. There must have been a hundred of them. Entire families bent on acquisition. Women with toddlers and old men with canes accompanying those who did the actual stealing. They swarmed over the ship. I didn't bother to hide. I wandered in a fog among them, all but unnoticed. Soon I felt lightheaded and I took a seat on a hatch cover. I must have passed out and someone must have noticed me then, for I woke that afternoon in Kaliaska. The following morning, a company plane flew me to Anchorage; two days later, another plane flew me to Stockholm. I haven't set foot on *Viator* since.

—Why not? Wilander asked. You came back to Alaska.

—I was many years in Sweden, attempting unsuccessfully to resurrect my career. The strain took a toll. I spent my health in the effort. *Viator* was always in my mind. I was convinced she was alive and wanted to understand her, to explore her. But I had no means of satisfying these ambitions. I worked for a nautical supply house. My commissions brought in scarcely enough for food and shelter. And then my parents died, passing within months of each other. My father had been prudent in his financial dealings, but the size of the inheritance was a shock for all that. I had the wherewithal to do anything I chose. My physical condition, however, was frail. I would not be able to endure life aboard a wrecked ship. I needed to be close to a decent medical facility.

A fishing boat steamed out from behind the headland, moving north and west, dark against the glittering blue water, heading—it appeared—for an empty quarter of the sea. Wilander felt an almost physical affinity with it. And so you came up with your plan, he said.

—There was nothing to keep me in Sweden. I had no children and my wife had initiated divorce proceedings as soon as she saw how things would go with my career. I flew to Alaska and bought the agency. And now I know I was right about everything.

—About *Viator* being alive?

—That...yes. And about the presentiment I had after we ran aground—that there was more to be done. More I had to do. I gave this short shrift in my story, but that feeling was stronger in me than any other I had during the entire experience. The company dragged me away so quickly, I had no opportunity to understand the role I was to play in *Viator*'s future. I knew she needed me. Whatever happened during the storm...and I'm not sure now the storm was significant. Or if it was, if it served to awaken the ship, no spirit came to us on its winds. I've come to think it was our lives, through some affinity, some freakish unity, that provided *Viator* with the energy she required to live. I believe she manipulated Kameus and the others to isolate me on board, so she could then direct me to run her aground in a specific place. I think her control over the five of us was imprecise and she needed to be precise in controlling me. For years I've believed as much, but I've had nothing to flesh out my belief. What you've told me makes everything comprehensible.

—I'm glad you comprehend it. I don't.

—It's not that I can explain any of it in rational terms, Lunde said. All events have a genuis. When two people meet and fall in love, it can be explained. Biology. Social reasons. But there's an inexplicable genius at its heart. We can't explain it, so many of us pretend we're being rational by ignoring it. You and I, though.... We realize the genius of certain events cannot be ignored. Somehow *Viator* became alive and saved herself from the breaking ground. She has lain dormant for twenty years, denied the energy she needed to continue on her way. By the time men returned to her decks, she had rusted. Her life, her newborn vitality, had rusted as well and it took her months to be revitalized. To make repairs. Well, she's made them and now she's on her way. Where she's bound, you have a better idea than I.

—I don't know, said Wilander.

—You doubt it, then? Even after hearing what I've told you?

—Do I doubt *Viator* is bound for...another world? Or that she's piercing a dimensional barrier? Those seem to be the options, don't they?

—I'm sure you have some degree of doubt. It would be impossible not to. But can you deny what's happening? I don't think so.

Wilander's anger, most of it, had been dissipated, diffused by his attentiveness, but now it resurfaced. I have to tell the others, he said stiffly. What they'll decide, I don't know. After that I'm going to pack and walk into Kaliaska.

—What will you do in Kaliaska?

—Not that it's your business, but I'm going to try and repair a relationship.

—With the Daupinee woman?

—How did you know that?

—She called the office some weeks ago. She made several calls, I believe. Judging by her manner, I thought there must be more than a casual involvement.

Wilander chose not to comment.

—One night at dinner, Lunde said. Not long after we met. You told me how as a child you dreamed of being an explorer, of standing in places where no man before you had stood. Do you remember?

—If you say so, Wilander said, amazed that he had been so open with Lunde; but then, thinking back to those days, he recalled with some revulsion how desperate he had been to get off the streets, out of the shelters, the missions, and his eagerness to be befriended, to be acquired as a charitable venture.

—Will you walk away from that dream when it is so close to fulfillment? Give it up for an ordinary life?

—Dreams change. Having any sort of life seems extraordinary to me now.

—Childhood dreams express the true depth of our desires. You can learn to make accommodations, to settle for less, but when such a dream offers itself, surely this is not your response?

—I'm not certain it is offering itself.

—I grant you, what lies ahead is unknown. There is risk, but it's one we all dare even if we're not daring by nature. The unknown is always with us.

—If you're convinced this is the right path, and you believe *Viator*'s truly on its way somewhere, why don't you join us? Why not reclaim your command? You won't have to endure a long wait now things have proceeded to this point.

—I would be pleased to join you, but the trip to Kaliaska might finish me off, Lunde said. I have a few months, they tell me. Less, perhaps.

The fishing boat had turned due west, dwindled to a speck, and the masses of clouds were also westering, as if the boat were towing them along on an invisible rope; the sky directly overhead was vacant, a pure wintry blue.

—I'm sorry, Wilander said, a comment that summarized an emotion more complicated and much less poignant than sorrow.

Lunde grunted in acknowledgement. As am I. Look, I'll pay you to stay on board. I'll pay you a lot of money.

—Why would you do that? You said you knew enough, your curiosity's satisfied.

—Perhaps because it's all that's left for me to do. And it would be pleasant to wake one morning and learn that *Viator* has vanished to another sea. That might reassure me as regards the nature of the voyage I'm soon to take. To tell the truth, I have so many reasons, you could likely construct a reason of your own and it would be at least partially correct.

—How much will you pay me?

—Twenty thousand.

—Fifty thousand, Wilander said. Put fifty thousand in

my account by tomorrow, and I'll consider staying.

—You'll consider it? I would expect a guarantee.

—That's a risk you'll have to take. In fact, I can assure you the money will have minimal impact on my decision...though it may have sufficient weight to make a difference. Give some money to the others, too. Ten thousand each.

—Why less for them?

—If things don't work out for us here, Wilander said, or they don't work out for me in Kaliaska, if we end up with nowhere to go, alone on this filthy wreck, I don't expect they'll need as much as I will to drink themselves to death.

NINE

"...Come here..."

Had he given it the least thought, Wilander might have anticipated the reactions of his shipmates on hearing Lunde's story. Arnsparger wanted to know if they would continue to be paid, and Halmus scoffed, saying, Why should I believe you? Or Lunde, for that matter? If that's really the story he told, what proof can you give me that it's the truth? I don't know what you're up to, either one of you, but I'm not buying it. Nygaard barely listened, sitting on the chair in Wilander's cabin, his attention commanded by a faucet handle he was holding, admiring it as if it were a chrome daisy with four petals, and as for Mortensen.... After giving up on finding him, Wilander was at the table in the officers' mess, idly working on his maps, feeling listless each time he engaged the idea of walking into Kaliaska, worrying that Arlene might turn him away, when Mortensen appeared in the door that opened onto the passageway, gaunt and ghastly looking, his shoulder-length hair matted, his beard begrimed, yet uncustomarily cheerful—he smiled as Wilander retold Lunde's story, ruining his image of revenant saintliness with a display of crooked brown teeth, looking instead as if he were the spiritual relic of an especially noisome odor or the astral guardian of a landfill, and once the story was complete, rather than responding to it, he poked at the maps with a bony, whitish-gray forefinger, like a parsnip in color, and praised Wilander for having devised so intriguing a destination (he had taken the liberty of studying the maps while Wilander was otherwise occupied), saying also that while he had doubted Wilander's suitability for the captain's cabin, he doubted it no longer. And when Wilander asked why he had used the word *devised*, Mortensen said, Didn't you listen to Lunde? It should be clear what's happened. The life force of Lunde and his officers fused with *Viator* during the storm. They were wedded to the instincts of the ship, her instinct to survive, to travel, just as the ship's life was ultimately wedded to the life of the forest. Since Lunde proved to be most in accord with her instincts, the ship chose him to plot the course of her survival. Now that you've taken Lunde's place, in union both with *Viator* and the forest, you're creating not only maps of the land to which we're traveling, but also the land itself, the (here he shuffled the maps about, peering at their legends)...the Iron Shore.

This astonishing recitation, so glibly delivered that it seemed practiced, left Wilander speechless.

—Arnsparger and Halmus view things somewhat differently, Mortensen went on. And yet I wouldn't call their views contrary. They're more complimentary, I'd say. Variant.

Still astonished, Wilander asked, You knew about the storm? And about Lunde?

—Not in so many words, but it was obvious something

like that had happened. It's happened to us, after all. Maybe you've been so wrapped up in your mapmaking, you haven't had the opportunity to step back and view the situation, but....

—You believe the maps, my maps, are making this place real?

Mortensen gave a sweeping gesture, like one a preacher might employ when enthusing about promised glories, and said, There are worlds of possibility out there. Real as mist. Your mind, in alliance with *Viator* and the forest, with their power, their steadfastness, is influencing one of those worlds to harden into physical form. The signs of its three creators are present in your maps. The forest, the sea, the city. Surely you can see it? Even Nygaard sees it in his simple-minded way. Every reality is given form by means of a similar consensus.

The conversation evolved into a lecture, a dissertation upon the topic of *Viator*, Whence, Whither, and Wherefore, Mortensen pointing out the resonances between Lunde's story and their experiences, and pointing out distinctions as well. He declared that the storm's fury and the power of the sea had served as a battery that enabled the forging of a bond between *Viator* and its previous crew, essentially the same that had been forged between *Viator* and themselves, yet it had taken longer to complete that second bond because there had been no crucible moment of wind and enormous waves, only the battery of slow time, and the union produced by this gradual process was stronger than the original, and necessarily so, for it was no simple passage that lay ahead, no few days of wind and sea, and great strength and endurance would be demanded of them. But the primary focus of his disquisition was upon the link between Lunde's charts and Wilander's maps, those acts of the imagination that had created and were creating an appropriate landfall for *Viator*. In response to Wilander's comment that, as far as he knew, the forest adjoining Kaliaska was not Lunde's creation, it had existed for centuries prior to Lunde's birth, Mortensen said, Yes, yet not in its current form; Lunde had authored a change that prepared the forest for *Viator*'s advent, a small thing when compared to Wilander's creation, to be sure, but Lunde's forest was the precursor of the Iron Shore, a stage in the journey, perhaps the first of many stages, and wasn't Wilander aware of the innumerable theories deployed about a single fundamental idea, that the observer creates reality?, my God, it was a basic tenet of philosophy, implicit in every philosophical paradigm, every religion, even Christianity, at least it had been part of the Christian belief system before the Council of Nicea scrubbed the doctrine clean of its Asiatic influences; and both the most primitive conceptions of universal order (sympathetic magic, for instance, the notion that a voodoo priest could heal a sick man by feeding a bull meal in which a drop or two of the patient's blood was mixed, forming a bond between animal and man that would permit the bull's vigor to subdue the disease) and the most sophisticated insights of physics (fractals, the behaviors of subatomic particles, etc.) gave evidence of the interconnectivity of all matter, and it was this interconnection that had permitted Lunde and Wilander to channel their energies with such efficacy; then Mortensen, with a triumphant expression, his point having been firmly established (to his own mind, at any rate), proceeded to embellish his theory, his estimation of the event that surrounded them, that had closed them in, by linking the concept of an observer-created reality with the phenomenon of crop circles, with the casting of spells, and thence with the summoning of demons, exorcisms, séances, the hierarchies of the angels, astrological conjunctions, with top-secret scientific breakthroughs known to nine anonymous men in the government and the Satanic strategies codified by the webs of certain South American spiders, with the entire catalogue of lunacy from which middle-class neurotics the world over selected the crutches that allowed them to walk the earth without crumbling beneath the merciless stare and brutal radiations of a god who was nothing like the images in the catalogue variously depicting him to be a gentle dreamy shepherd, a mighty bearded apparition, an architect of fate (*God's Blueprint For YOUR Heavenly Mansion* by Dr. Carter P. Zaslow, $22.95 plus shipping), a universe-sized vessel of love; and after Mortensen ended his discourse and returned to the shadowy places of *Viator*, Wilander, who had been halfway convinced by the initial portion of his remarks, realized that Mortensen's mad-prophet pose masked a pitiful, ordinary madness, the madness that had doubtless afflicted him while abusing himself with fortified wine on the streets of several Alaskan cities; and, recognizing that he could trust not a word that had been said by either Mortensen or Lunde, he made a rashly considered call to Arlene, told Lunde's story yet again, and asked her to check out the details on the Internet. She replied frostily that she would if she could find the time (she called back a day later, at an hour when he typically shut off his phone, and left a message saying that she had substantiated the basics of the story—the survival of the crew, Lunde's dismissal, and so on—and that she had asked a hacker friend in the Forty-Eight to do a more thorough search) and said she didn't believe this qualified as an emergency, she did not want him calling whenever he got nervous, did he understand?, okay then, goodbye. And Wilander, feeling isolated to an unparalleled degree—even sleeping alone beneath a cardboard sheet in an alley, he had heard voices, traffic, and known himself to be still part of the human sphere, but here there was only the silence and inhuman vibration of the ship—stepped out onto the deck and discovered that an inch of snow had fallen and more was coming down, big wet flakes that promised a heavy accumulation, yet vanished when they touched his palm, and he was so affected by this consolation of nature, by the whiteness of the deck, by the soft hiss of the snowfall, by the smell of heaven it brought, he stood with his face turned to the sky, watching with childish fascination as the flakes came spinning out of the incomprehensible dark, letting them melt and trickle down his cheeks like the tears of a vast immaterial entity who—eyeless and full of sorrows—had seen fit to use a lesser being to manifest its weeping.

* * *

With the snow came bitter cold, and by week's end *Viator* was resplendent in a glittering drag of ice and snow, an old battered queen overdressed for a ball, wearing every bit of gaud in her closet, ice sheathing the rails, plating the decks, icicles descending from the toppled winch, from every protruding edge, and the forest, too, was shrouded in white—although during even the worst of the weather, a blizzard lasting for almost two days, the fir trunks and sprays of blackish green needles showed amid the whiteness like splotches of dark metal on a wall from which the paint was flaking—and as the snow continued, Wilander would glimpse flashes of corruscant light emitted by an indeterminate source in the middle distance and hear the complaint of tortured metal, a display he associated not with *Viator*'s penetration of the Kaliaskan shore twenty years previously, but with a new penetration, one just begun, made by a ghostly prow. Though he alternated between fear and disbelief in regard to what appeared be happening to *Viator*, he had given up the thought of abandoning the ship. For one thing, Arlene's manner made it plain there was nothing for him in town, and for another, the forest was alive with surreptitious movement, with the cries of the qwazil, with other, unfamiliar cries, and something large had taken up residence in the linden tree (against logic, it had retained its leaves, although they had gone brown and papery and were now beginning to fall), shaking down snow showers whenever it moved, and he had on several occasions spotted what appeared to be multiple tracks on the shingle. But the most telling reason behind his reluctance to leave was a vacant, unstudied disaffection with the idea, a non-reason that eventually translated into a sense that he was better off where he was, that life in a fantasy of his design, albeit one whose existence he did not wholly credit, was preferable to anything he might encounter elsewhere. And once he embraced this passive choice, a spark of certainty was kindled by his every smaller choice, as if by staying he had come to terms with all life's problems; and perhaps Halmus and Arnsparger and Nygaard had achieved a similar peace of mind, for the atmosphere aboard ship was cordial by contrast to what had gone before, with pleasantries and nods and brief, cheerful dialogues exchanged in passing; and, after the storm blew off, the diamond weather that followed seemed an additional validation that a sea change had taken place—long perfect days of white sunbursts in pale blue skies; hushed, enduring twilights that washed the snow lavender; blue nights with haloed moons and hard bright stars when Wilander, alone with his maps, felt like a magus imprisoned in a crystal, laboring over a casting that would set him free, detailing the coastlines of the Six Tears, adding a notch to the tip of the peninsula that bordered the lagoon, putting the finishing touches on the city of Cape Lorraine, adding marginalia beside portions of the forests, noting a concentration of whistlers or some other imaginary creature, not quite believing the fantasy, playing with it, obsessive in the way of a hobbyist or a gamer, and yet telling himself maybe, perhaps, what if, supposing it were real, tempted to belief. Sometimes he would walk out into the forest (not far; he remained uneasy with the environment) in order to gain a perspective on the ship, to think whatever thoughts the sight of it would generate, contemplating it as might a connoisseur in a gallery, the moonstruck superstructure, so pristine looking, a clean light spilling from ports and doors, here and there a refracted crystalline glint, and the sharp black prow lifting from between hills and boulders as if cleaving a swell, a far cry from the brooding image it had once presented, resembling a stranded luxury craft wherein a party of minor dukes and their be-gemmed ladies, confident of rescue, quietly celebrated the moment with the roast flesh of mythical beasts and wine fermented centuries before by eunuch saints in a Serbian castle; and one night, returning from a walk, as he clambered over the aft rail, having shinnied up the frozen rope from the shingle, he saw a shadow drop to the deck from the linden tree. At that distance, he could determine only that the shadow was human. He crept closer, keeping low to the rail, more intrigued than frightened, imagining that it must be someone from town. The shadow flattened against the outer wall of the officers' mess and had a peek in through the port. Wilander would not have sworn to it, but the face that flared for an instant in the light from the port appeared to be that of a woman with extremely long hair. Then, as he crept closer yet, placing his feet carefully so as not to crunch patches of ice, she opened the door of the mess and stepped into the light, proving to be a slender young girl, dirty blonde hair falling over her shoulders and down her back; utterly naked, her skin onion pale, small-breasted, her crotch all but hairless; and then she darted inside, leaving the door ajar. Easing forward again, Wilander found an angle that allowed him to peer into the mess. The girl moved with furtive quickness about the table, and perhaps, he thought, she was no girl—although her body exhibited the immature development of a fourteen-year-old, her face was exotic, womanly, a beautiful, sensual face with high cheekbones and a mouth that was a little too wide and full for her narrow jaw. She pawed at the maps, stopped and tipped back her head as if catching a scent on the air; she picked up a colored pencil, bit it, tossed it aside, sniffed the air again, and then sped through the door leading to interior of the ship. Dumbfounded, Wilander held his position. Rather than pursuing her through the darkened maze of the ship, he thought it would be easier to intercept her when she returned to the mess; but as he debated whether it would be more effective to wait inside the mess, she sprinted back onto the deck, carrying a loaf of bread, leaped to the rail without breaking stride and vaulted up into the linden, bringing down a shower of snow and dead leaves. An air of unreality settled over Wilander. That a beautiful woman might be inhabiting the linden tree, existing in freezing temperatures without the benefit of clothing, failed to meet even his lowered standards of what was credible. Unless she were a whistler, in which case the very concept of judgment would take a hit. Shy; slender; physically alluring. Driven to steal food when winter made game scarce. She fit the description. He started for the larder, curious as to how she had negotiated the lock, and then recalled that he had bread, peanut butter, and tinned sardines in his cabin. The sardines and peanut butter, he discovered, were still on the shelf above his bunk. The bread, however, was gone. Over the next few weeks, Wilander devoted considerable thought and energy toward the woman in the linden tree, putting aside his maps (they were more or less complete) and his concerns relating to the white lights and the noises and the increasingly active, albeit still-invisible population of the forest. Since a normal woman could never withstand such cold, and since her behavior suggested an animal intelligence, he was persuaded that she must be a whistler, and he set himself to capture her, leaving food out to lure her down from the tree, hoping to habituate her to the process and eventually trap her in the mess; but the next night, watching from hiding as she secured the block of cheese he had provided, he became aroused by the play of muscles in her thighs and abdomen, by facial features whose delicacy seemed evidence of a sensitivity belied by her primitive actions. It troubled him that he could feel desire for anyone other than Arlene, whom he loved despite the breach between them. The whistler was unquestionably a beautiful creature, but first and foremost she was a creature; it dismayed him to suspect that he might be engaged in so prurient a self-deception, but what purpose apart from the sexual would trapping her serve? The phrase with which Halmus had insulted him, *the husband of the linden tree*: It returned to Wilander now and he wondered if—given Mortensen's theories—he had summoned the whistler from the uncreate to fulfill the odd promise of that phrase. He decided that he would befriend her, not attempt a capture, and he placed food at the end of the table nearest the outer door and sat at the opposite end, waiting to see what would happen. For three successive nights, he heard her tread on the deck, yet she declined to enter. On the fourth night, however, she slipped into the mess, snatched the food and, as she darted away, in a panic, she smacked into the edge of the door, causing it to slam shut, trapping her. She whirled about, pursed her lips; he felt a pinprick of pain behind his forehead, but it faded, amounting to nothing. He made soothing noises, urging her to calm, and stood, intending to close the interior door (he didn't want her loose in the ship) and then open the outer door, allowing her to escape; but as he moved to accomplish this, she dropped to her hands and knees, presenting him her hindquarters, plainly a sexual offering. A second later, he smelled a sweetly complex scent, reminiscent of the sachets his mother had strewn about their home, seeking to mask odors that only she detected (the taint of a failing marriage, the residue of his father's affairs) with tiny cloth bundles containing dried flowers, and he was struck by the thought that although he and his parents had never gotten along, though they had not even liked each other, it was weird how infrequently they sprang to mind.... The scent, more cloying than those remembered scents, dizzied him. He gazed at the whistler's pale buttocks. What would be wrong, he asked himself, if he were to fuck this consenting animal childwoman, this fantasy figure who he had dialed up from his subconscious? What possible significance could morality and conscience have when everything he imagined was coming true? Sufficient, it seemed, to restrain him. Still dizzy, he sat down again. The whistler got to one knee, staring at him, her torso partly concealed beneath tangles of hair. Wilander gestured at the door. You opened it before, he said. Go. She came slowly into a half-crouch, reached behind her, groping for the door, keeping her eyes on him. He told her once more to go, his tone peremptory, and, with a lunge, shouldering the door as she wrestled with the bar, she flung herself out onto the deck and, judging by the furious rustling that ensued, scrambled high into the linden tree.

Two nights passed before she entered the mess again, and two nights after that, a particularly cold night, with the temperature hovering near zero, a thousand glittering daggers of ice hung like trophies about *Viator*'s deck, a half moon whose light at meridian was so strong that a portion of the ice-sheathed railing at the stern looked to be a curve of gemmy fire suspended against the less focused brightness of the sea beyond, it was then that Aralyn—this the name Wilander had given the whistler, the name of a cousin in Goteberg whom he had never met—crouched in a corner of the mess while she ate the chicken breast he had set out for her; and the night after that she balked at returning to the linden tree. Not only was the cold affecting her (she had been trembling when she entered, making her seem even younger, frailer, like the little match girl), but the leaves of the linden had thinned out over the past days to such a degree, it no longer served as an effective hiding place, and this provided a clue to the size of the qwazil, who continued to call from the uppermost branches, secreted behind a smallish spray of leaves, marking itself as a tiny bird with a big voice...or else, like the wiccara, it was invisible. With both gesture and word, Wilander encouraged Aralyn to leave, but she curled up on the floor under the table as if she planned to sleep there; though it was unlikely that any of the crew would have reason to enter the mess during the night, it was nevertheless a possibility, and Wilander did not trust that they would have as protective an attitude toward her as he—she hadn't filled the hole in his life that Arlene had left, nothing could, but her presence cut the loneliness to a more tolerable level, and he was coming to dote on her, to think of her as something of a cross between a niece and a pet; he made notes on her height and weight (a shade over five feet, slightly less than a hundred pounds) and physical condition (healthily sinewed; skin unmarred except for a pink two-inch-long scar shaped like a smile under her right breast; large eyes with dark irises and clear whites), and also noted how clean she was aside from her snarled hair and wondered if she washed herself like a cat or, as with certain breeds of dog, Samoyeds and Akitas, if she had a naturally pleasing odor. He indulged in a serial daydream in which, after reaching the Iron Shore, leaving *Viator* to sail unknown seas alone and un-captained, a living ship bent upon her own fulfillment, he became the great protector of the whistlers, a figure part Moses, part Che Guevara, part Martin Luther King, and pictured himself standing with Aralyn at the forefront of a host of whistlers, all dressed in homespun robes, freshly civilized, the forest ranked behind them, gazing with ennobled mein across a vista rife with promise. Okay, he told her. But you can't stay here. And again with word and gesture, he urged her into the passageway and along it to his cabin, where, after displaying some signs of anxiety, she finally settled on the floor and slept. Wilander lay awake, listening to her breath, recognizing that he was establishing a dangerous precedent—she couldn't stay in the cabin, or maybe she could, maybe it would be for the best; and if *Viator* was, indeed, on her way to the ultimate elsewhere, another plane of existence, a world he may have created, then she wouldn't have to stay for long, no more than a week if the nearness of the lights and the increased volume of the groaning were indicators; and in the midst of these considerations, he fell asleep, a sleep undisturbed by dreams, unless waking to find himself enveloped in sweetness, a complex perfume, and Aralyn's fingers stroking him, making him hard, unless all that were a dream, and he came up from the fog of sleep, meaning to push her away, but when he touched her, his disgust—a flicker—was subsumed by desire, his hands clamped to her flesh, and then she was rising above him, a shadow in the dark, fitting herself to him, just the way Arlene liked, only Arlene enjoyed sitting astride him and touching herself, whereas this one, Aralyn, was erratic in her movements, clawing at his chest, and that was his last clinical thought until after he had spilled into her and lay stiff with self-loathing, bothered by the weight of her head on his chest, her hand on his stomach, but unwilling now to push her away, to treat her roughly, because it wasn't her fault, she had merely been trying to protect herself after having wandered into this unfamiliar place through a cosmic rip in the walls of her world made by *Viator*'s push to survive, acting on instinct...though it was possible, he realized, that he had assumed incorrectly, that he underestimated the whistlers and they were not sub-humans, not creatures of animal instinct, but fully human, a variant form of the species. In an effort to validate this thesis, he managed to teach Aralyn to say *Tom* and *food,* but since she banged on the floor with the candy bar he had used to illustrate *food* (mimicking the frustration he had displayed while teaching her) whenever she said the word, he couldn't be sure she understood its meaning, nor was he sure—*if* she understood, *if* her intellect was more advanced than he had thought—whether this would put him in the clear ethically speaking. He doubted it would. Ethics had not been a strong point of his for many years.

The weather dirtied up, cluttered gray skies, snow flurries driven by offshore winds, dazzling explosions of light, like huge photic rips in the landscape, no more than fifteen or twenty yards ahead of the prow, and the din of metal under stress grew so articulated, Wilander could imagine the precise injuries being done, the iron plates gouged, dimpling, tearing. Wind howled about the ship; fir trees dumped loads of old snow onto the decks, and snow blew across the shingle, building drifts against the boulders. At night they would go into the mess for an hour or so and during that time Aralyn would run outside, probably to do her business—he hadn't attempted to instruct her on the use of the toilet—while he leafed through his maps, adding a detail or two, wondering if they were accurate, and after she returned, they would return to the cabin. Lunde called on Friday morning to hear his report (Wilander having failed to call) and, recognizing the number on his caller ID, not wanting to talk, Wilander switched off the phone and left it off. If they were leaving the Alaskan Coast, and he could no longer harbor any reasonable doubt that they were, he did not wish to spend his last minutes on earth supplying Lunde with a blow-by-blow account of the passage, committed to routine like an astronaut. He sat brooding on his bunk, despairing of himself for having traded in a decent life with Arlene for a trip to nowhere with this womanly animal, who was playing with a candy wrapper on the floor. A pretty animal, an animal who appeared to be naturally housebroken, a relatively intelligent animal, yet not a terrific conversationalist. She had forgotten *Tom*, but every so often she would smile, a smile whose seductive quality was neutralized by the vacancy in her eyes, and say, Food. They had only engaged in sex the once, but that night Wilander, who had reminisced about Arlene much of the day, tormenting himself with the idea of abandoning *Viator*, knowing he would never do it, came to feel so desolate that he could no longer psychically afford to give weight to the question of whether or not he was debasing himself—he wanted to lose track, to forget *Viator*, forget Halmus, Arnsparger, Nygaard, Mortensen, to forget Arlene, and he beckoned to Aralyn and patted the blanket beside him. Either she did not understand or she chose not to comply.

—Come here, he said, patting the blanket harder.

Squatting on the floor, her bare arms and legs sticking out from what could have passed for a ratty shawl and a vest of dirty blond hair, she looked like a feral child, and, though he realized she could alter her expression by a shade and then seem much less the savage innocent, that didn't soften the comprehension of what he was doing, and he felt a distant displeasure, angry that she was forcing him to control her. He shouted, slapped the blankets, and that confused her. At length he dragged her onto the bunk beside him and showed her how a zipper worked—not that she would retain the information—and pushed her head down, hoping that she knew what came next. She did. Clever girl. But as he lay back, shutting his eyes, he saw the photograph that was about to be mounted in his permanent scrapbook, the shot that would fix for all time the image of derelict ex-human living in the shell of a wrecked ship with other derelicts and getting sex from a creature who was a pedophile's wet dream and had less than a room temperature IQ, a photograph so vivid, he could smell his own decaying spirit, the soul rotting in the rotten flesh, and he went limp, shoved her to the end of the bunk, where she sat a moment bewildered, spittle on her lips, then tried to crawl up beside him, and he shoved her back again, cursed at her until she scooted down onto the floor, huddling in a corner by the sink, staring fearfully at him. Tears started from Wilander's eyes and he understood that the emotional sponsor of those tears was neither regret nor loss, but a febrile self-pity based on a knowledge of what he was becoming. That daydream of his, playing Moses to the whistlers' Israelites, he envisioned it differently now; he pictured himself reclining on a mattress of boughs, surrounded by whistler women, using them whenever the mood struck, eating the berries and meat they brought him, the lord of a flyblown forest kingdom, purveyor of a petty colonialism, his hair lengthening to a moss-like robe from which his penis would occasionally protrude; growing older and weaker until he could do nothing more than digest a few berries and wait in dread for the whistlers, gone past innocence under his tutelage, to kill him with their teeth or the flint knives he'd taught them to make so they could be more efficient in the hunt. He flicked off the light and turned onto his side, facing the walls, wishing the world would hurry up and end. He thought he had been another kind of man once, basically good, not perfect, but he couldn't remember how it had felt. The wind gnawed at the iron bones of the ship, its harsh voice falling silent for an instant as if it were choking, having to dislodge a fragment from its throat, maybe a chunk of *chian* or *schaumere,* and then began to feast again.

TEN
"...what about Mortensen..."

He woke to the absence of wind, of all sound, the port enclosing a circle of pewter morning light, and, sitting up, rubbing his eyes, he registered the absence of Aralyn. The cabin door stood ajar. He felt a pang in his chest, knowing that he had frightened her away, but immediately thereafter felt relieved and hoped she had gone. He splashed water on his face, changed into fresh underwear, a clean shirt, a little worried that there was no sound, no groaning metal—not that the sound was continuous, it was intermittent, *Viator* forging ahead, then storing up more energy, forging ahead again, shattering the barrier in stages, but lately, more often than not, he woke to the groaning and he worried that *Viator* might have run out of energy, that they would be stuck and how much would that suck?, fuck, fuck, fuck.... He straightened out his thoughts from the skid they'd been in and saluted his image in the mirror, *Bon soir, mon capitan!*, and went briskly along the passageway to the mess. Which was a mess, coincidentally. His maps strewn about the floor and the outer door wide open, doubtless left so by Aralyn in her haste, letting in the wind. He bent a knee, prepared to start picking them up, but an animal chill touched the back of his neck and he straightened, suspecting that something was wrong. He stepped out onto the deck. The air was warmer, the icicles were beading at their tips, the snow underfoot was mushy, melting, and it was difficult to read the tracks, but there looked to be two sets of footprints leading to the stern. A soft grunting came to his ears. Perhaps some other animal wandered away from the Iron Shore. Wilander grew cautious in his approach, edging along the bulkhead. The grunting stopped. He paused, listening, and when it did not resume, he eased forward again, more of the stern coming into view, more yet, still more, and finally he spotted a gray-haired man standing facing the aft rail some thirty feet away, buckling his belt. Nygaard? Aralyn was there as well, creeping away along the rail until Nygaard barked at her, slapped her, raised his hand, threatening another slap, and she cowered. Wilander took in her chastened attitude and Nygaard's masterful pose. He gave a cry, a feeble thing, it sounded as if he'd been shot in the lung, and charged, tripped, went sprawling on the icy deck. Aralyn broke for the starboard, passing from view, and Nygaard made a scuttling run forward, his face registering a comical degree of panic; then he retreated and flung himself over the rail.

By the time Wilander regained his feet and staggered to the rail, Nygaard was down the rope and off into the forest. After the briefest of hesitations, he followed, furious at the little man for his transgression, for having befouled his woman, and he debated the truth of that as he went; he wondered if Nygaard might only be convicted of abusing a pet, but no, Wilander thought, catching sight of him heading over a rise (there you are, weaselly little shit), then passing out of sight.... No, these were frontier circumstances, frontier laws must therefore apply. They hung horsethieves, sheepstealers, why not whistler-fuckers? He envisioned himself calling Nygaard to judgment—Nygaard would back away, stumble in the snow, put out his hands in defense, say something pitiable, and Wilander, looming above him, would say, I pronounce...I pronounce.... Well, he would say something appropriate, something that would terrify Nygaard, that by its grandeur would infect him with dread, and then he would be on him with his fists flying, with kicks, goal-scoring kicks, delving in under the ribs, digging out his bones. As he floundered up the rise behind which Nygaard had vanished, a burst of light and noise, there came a shrieking and an accompanying flare of brightness that held and held, and he sank to his knees in the snow, stoppering his ears and squeezing his eyes shut. After an interminable time, the sound and light abated. He struggled to his feet and trudged to the top of the rise. Nygaard's trail gave out in a patch of disturbed snow. Another burst of light and noise, farther away, off to his right, caused Wilander to grit his teeth. With *Viator* so near to leaving, the forest was full of stress points and Nygaard must have stumbled directly into one. He would have to be very careful; he did not want to pass through the barrier without the ship. Without her iron keel, the great stress-bearer to surround him, he had little chance of survival. Yet Aralyn, the qwazil and the wiccara, they had slipped through safely. He struggled with the idea, considering the notion of two-way travel, pro-and-conning, trying out the idea that passage one way was easier than passage the other, and, giving it up as too problematic, he began hiking back to the ship. It was tough going in the snow, the air turning to ice in his lungs, and as he paused to catch his breath, he was transfixed by the sight of *Viator*. The overcast had deepened, big snowflakes swirling down, and the ship, trapped between the two confining hills, looked to be straining forward, shouldering its burden of ice and snow, battered and indefatigable, every splotch, every dent, every evidence of its long labor, visible in that neutral light. He felt a unity with her, a shared principle, an inelegant workers' purpose; they persevered, they hung in, they did their job. Tears came to his eyes on seeing his sister so resolute and undaunted. He glanced heavenward, less an emotional response than an involuntary attempt to clear his airway, and there, making a great soundless sweep across the lower sky was the creature of his dreams, the ropy wormlike thing, thrillingly vast, skimming the fir tops, clear for a split-second, a mile of gristle given definition by a central nub, leaving stillness in its wake. Wilander did not know what to do, dismasted by the sight. The firs had not bent beneath it, he had felt no great wind, so perhaps he had not seen it, perhaps he had fallen asleep in the snow and was dreaming. But the passage of the creature seemed a statement of finality. There was nothing left to do or say. He waited to be gathered, to wink out of existence, for some momentous event to occur. When it became clear that he was not to be taken, that this was not his time, only then did he collect the litter of self, the human stupidities, cram them back into his head, abandoning what would not fit, and went stumping through the snow toward *Viator*, not a thought in his head apart from that passage, that godlike passage, replaying it until the dark brown shadow it had cast became a dark brown cast of mind.

VIATOR

* * *

From the shingle, *Viator*'s hull was a brutish thing, black and blunt and patchy with ice, given a strangely delicate accent by the two crumpled screws with their defining crusts of snow, like two sugar flowers popping out from the belly of an unsodded grave; and there was an odd thing, as well, on the shore, a length of seaweed, iron in color, bulky, roughly man-sized, uncovered by the snow. Wilander's path led away from it, but he let his feet stray him near and found that it was not seaweed as it had appeared, but rust; a man made of rust. On peering closer, he recognized that man to be Arnsparger. Fright drove him back a step. He had a second look. The body was fully clothed, the clothes cunningly fashioned of rust; arranged lying on its stomach, its arms held close, face to the side, gaping—it might have fallen from the stern. Arnsparger must have put it there to be found, a grisly piece of art, but artful nonetheless. Wilander knelt by the body. The detail was exquisite. All of *ozim*. Here was Arnsparger's pen protruding from his trouser pocket; here the bulge of his wallet, the buttons on his shirt collar. He had not believed him capable of such. Beery, bluff Arnsparger, born in tavern light to a crowbar and keg of beer...he had done this? This miracle? How had he managed to fix the surface? Or did he, like the purest of artists, intend his work to be sacrificed, victimized by wind and weather? Wilander positioned his finger over Arnsparger's jowly, stupefied face, then thought, no, not the face, he wouldn't be the one to spoil the face, and, choosing an area near the belt, where the damage would not be so noticeable, he pushed in his finger. To his dismay, it went in easily. Ah, well. He withdrew it. Sheathed in rust, tipped in blood. He stared. Delicate flakes of red and black coated the finger from the knuckle to the first joint, giving way to glistening red. The fact of it sank in, as did the fact of a red leakage from the hole he had made. Something inside the figure settled, some imbalance registered, and its cheek caved in, rust leaked from an eyesocket. He jumped up and ran, nearly running up the rope, a mad scramble, flung himself over the rail, and made for the cabins, calling to Mortensen, to Halmus, wanting to alert them to a danger, but what was the danger? You couldn't yell, *Arnsparger's turned into rust!* and expect the same reaction you got by yelling, *Fire!* You would leave yourself open to ridicule, and rightly so. Mortensen wasn't in his cabin; he must be down in the hold and he could rot there, because Wilander wasn't poking his nose in the hold, no sir, not on his life, and he burst into Halmus' cabin, noticing the glass had been knocked out of the port just as his feet skidded out from under him—he squawked, flailed, slammed down, knocking the back of his head painfully, not losing consciousness, squeezing his eyes against the pain. After the pain subsided he saw that the port glass was littering the floor and one of the crumbs, a chunk the size of a marble, held part of a brown eye. He thought it was reflecting his eye until he remembered his eyes were blue. Groggily, he sat up, bracing against the bottom of Halmus' bunk. Turned the piece over in his hand. It showed the same from every angle, as if the eye were turning with it, interested in him. Wilander was too exhausted to register much of a reaction. Another chunk held the corner of a sneering mouth, and another a section of neatly trimmed beard. He had gone a ways toward assembling Halmus' face before deciding he did not want to see the expression he had worn at the moment of death. Scattering the death mask on the floor, crunching the pieces underfoot, he walked along the passageway to his cabin and lay down on his bunk. Something dug into his back. The cell phone. He switched the thing on. Lots of messages, but he didn't have a lot to say, just he wished this trip was over, Sayonara, and like that. He was tired, too full of angles for which there were no.... The thought tailed off, uncompleted. He couldn't count, he couldn't think. His phone rang. Watching the little dingus vibrating on his chest made for a fun few seconds, but soon grew tiresome. It stopped. Seconds later it rang again. He picked it up, said, Hello.

—Thomas? I've been trying to reach you. Where've you been?

Around the world and back again.

—Hey...Arlene! He was genuinely happy to hear her voice.

—Listen, she said. That friend of mine, the hacker? I sent him what you told me....

—How are you? Are you okay?

—Thomas! You have to get off the ship! There's a chance....

—I've really missed you.

She spoke to someone, her conversation muted, then said, The Fat Allie out of Mayorkiq. You remember? The fishing boat that Lunde told you about. There is no Mayorkiq, not anymore. The....

—Do you miss me?

—Yes. Yes, I miss you. The people in Mayorkiq, they went crazy, they all died except for two or three. They sent a....

—I love you.

That gave her pause, but then not for long. A science team went in and found these crates, she said. Nobody knew where they came from....

—Arlene?

—Its obvious now they came from *Viator*. They contained an engineered virus.

—I want to fuck you, he said gleefully.

—This is serious, Thomas! That thing you're always drawing? That thing in your dreams? That's it!

—The...what?

—The virus! That thing you've been dreaming about. There's a picture of it the web page he sent me. The crates must have cracked open. You've got to get off the ship! We're on our way out, Terry and me....

Sternly, he said, I thought we'd settled that.

—What?

—I'm not leaving.

—Haven't you been listening? You're at risk!

—You can't expect me to leave now...now we're so close.

—God, Thomas! Don't you understand! Everything that's happened is the fault of that fucking ship!

He sat up, swung his legs off the bunk. Not everything...not everything's the fault of that fucking ship! You turned into an animal! You didn't have to do that! An animal! That wasn't the ship's fault, that wasn't the ship's fault!!

—Thomas, please. I'm just....

Viator

—You keep telling me to leave! You keep telling me! Well, why don't you try it, huh? Why don't you try! Ahhh...fuck!

He threw the phone at the wall, satisfied to watch it splinter into little plastic bones, and sank back on the bed, emptied by rage, empty of hope, of vitality, of delirium—he could make a long list of the things he was empty of; and for a while he checked off this item and that, yes, yes, no, almost, and it got to be like counting sheep, he tried to sleep, but the sound and light were almost constant, and he just lay there, listening to the groaning, watching the flashes of light, so vivid, so pure a white he could see every color in them, see anything he wanted, and he wanted to see Arlene, she wasn't really angry at him, she was sad he was leaving, and it saddened him to be leaving. He had a long, cool thought of her, an eyes-closed thought of how she'd drag her pendulant breasts over his chest, and when he opened his eyes she was sitting astride him, her red hair undone, in all her full, sweet, hot life, but as for him, his chest was bones, just a ribcage and shriveled heart and lungs within, and he wasn't shocked, the image tired him, but he wasn't shocked, because he was leaving, she was staying; it was the voice of hallucinatory reason warning him away from things he could not have. He replaced her with the whistler. The queen of Kaliaska replaced by a kitten with vacant eyes who made lustful cooing noises; but at least his chest had been restored. The weight of his thoughts dragged him under the ground of sleep and into a dream; he was back in school, something about acorns, Bliss put in an appearance, as did Arlene and a giant, and then he woke to a prolonged grating shudder, to the signal long awaited, of *Viator* getting under way.

Feeling creaky in his joints, Wilander stumbled along the passage and came out into light which, though gray, absent all but a tin-colored smear of sun, hurt his eyes, out into blustery weather, snow flurries driven by gusts of wind, and just ahead of the prow, no more than a few feet, a dazzling corona twice the height of the ship, flaring and dwindling, every few seconds opening to reveal a view of another coast, a different view each time, as if *Viator* were choosing the perfect point of entry onto the Iron Shore, and they were edging forward, inch by painful inch—he could feel the living skin of her tormented by the pressure of rock, accompanied by groans, shrieks, shrill sounds of metal swelling and constricting, pushed through a narrows like no other, and he staggered, caught the rail, peering out into the coronal depths, at Cape Lorraine, at the sweep of the virgin forest, at all the wonders of that new world, and felt life pour through him, *Viator*'s life and his, they shared a heart, or rather his heart was *Viator*'s laboring engine, embarked upon a journey to end all journeys. He'd been wrong to picture his life ending in ignominy, wrong in his conjuring of days and nights spent in the forest with the whistlers; he would stay aboard *Viator*, remain her captain and sail the seas (more than seven by his reckoning), traverse the globe, going from port to port, and once they'd done the tour, once they'd gone from Cape Lorraine to Port Satine—the name came unbidden to his tongue, with a promise attached of wild tropics, talking statues, golden birds, distinguished gentlemen with exotic secrets to convey, enchanted prisoners with whispered tales of worse than life, blind wizards, black princesses, back-stair madonnas who would drain the poisons from a sailor's flesh with their perfect lips and work their spittle into white beads they sold as remedies—why not another world, another escape, why not go on and on? Ceaselessly, tirelessly. A glorious future was to be theirs, Columbus' dream of heaven, the voyage of endless discovery. And then Mortensen, Saint Mortensen, a ragged figure, his beard wider than his chest, ran into the bow just as the image of the coast of Multikelio appeared in the corona, just as fire began to chew iridescent sparks from the prow. He shouted something, but there was too much din too hear, and he smiled, a fiercely enjoining smile, and, turning to the prow, to the light of his salvation, addressing the fire as he might his deliverer, with his arms outspread, he let it wash over him.

    The fire continued eating the ship inch by inch, the groaning and shrieking grew louder, and Wilander, aghast at this act of self-immolation, made less certain of his fate, backed away, backed until he could back no more, and sat down heavily in the stern. He thought he should do something, but could think of nothing and so began to weep, to sob as *Viator*, shuddering violently, launched into an unfathomed sea. As the fire devoured the collapsed winch and reached the verge of the superstructure, he hid his face in his hands and wept. He did not know why he wept—it seemed a matter of convenience that he not know and so he wept for the sadness of not knowing. Then hands were laid on him, soft hands, Arlene's hands; Arlene and Terry, cluttering his thoughts with their daft fumbling, their clumsy touches. What could they want? He had nothing for them. He doubted their existence, they were ghosts, demons come to tempt him. He pulled away, clambered to his feet, and stood unsteadily, his legs miles long and swaying. They tried to encircle him, to pen him in, and he fended them off with wild swings of his fists, weeping all the while. They spoke words he could not hear, yet knew were entreaties. He glanced at the fire. Forty feet away. He started for it, heard Arlene shout his name, and saw her standing with arms outstretched, face broken with fear. He took a step toward her, intending to console, to remedy, and it seemed in that step were all the steps he had ever taken, all the missteps, all the firm first steps, all the steps leading to good and evil, only this one had no ending, no landfall, and he pitched downward, falling into a pool of blackness like a sailor who had mistaken a puddle of rain for the sea.

* * *

Over the fifty-nine days of his confinement in a military hospital, Wilander pieced together a story that, like any story, had its flaws, its holes, but sufficed to encompass more or less the facts of which it was made. *Viator*'s cargo, unlisted on the manifest, consisted of two containers of a virus as yet unnamed *(It's a lentivirus, actually. Maybe we'll name it for you, huh?)*, a Russian bioweapon, one of which had cracked open in Lunde's storm and polluted the hold. Perhaps it had been intended to be destroyed with the ship, but this was thought unlikely; more likely, it had been meant for terrorist hands. The lentivirus bonded with DNA in brain neurons, gradually driving the host mad *(You're going to have to put up with this bad boy for a while, but we'll keep him calm with drugs)*. Halmus and Arnparger had been dead for weeks and days respectively when he happened upon them. Everything he had seen and experienced on the ship was, after a certain point, fantasy. The gigantic lentivirus of his dreams, his madness? They mumbled some business about impingement on the optic nerve and told him not to worry about it.

—But what about Mortensen? he asked. And Nygaard...what about him?

—Who knows? I guess they ran off in the woods somewhere, was the answer.

Wilander came in time to believe the story, to have faith in it as much as he had faith in anything; not much, but he felt he should have faith because so many people told him it was true, and thus he yielded to it, he rejected fantasy and let it soothe him. Still frail and uncertain, he was discharged into Arlene's care and together they returned to Kaliaska. Thanks to the madness of the late Jochanan Lunde, he did not need to work, but he helped out at the trading post as he felt able and things fell into a routine. One afternoon in the dead of winter, straight past the turn of the year, he borrowed Terry's launch and motored out to *Viator*, anchoring just offshore. Under gray skies; sheeted with ice; steeped in the gloomy shadow of the firs; she no longer seemed haunted, merely abandoned, and this effect was amplified by the lifelessness of the sea, the listless wash of black water against the sides of the launch, and by the great stillness of the scene, not a breath of wind to stir the needles and dump fresh snow on the decks, to snap the icicles, to breed a ghostly moan. The screws did not resemble crumpled flowers, but twisted metal, and the hull, which had once struck him as bloated, now was dented, derelict, empty. Biohazard teams had cut the heart from her, hosing down the hold with chemicals, and left her flensed and gutted. She looked like a place where men had gone mad. Wilander had seen enough, but was reluctant to leave, and he sat for the better part of an hour, lulled to a dreamy self-regard by the rocking of the launch, thinking about fate, how it was deemed capricious and yet was clearly insane—it went beyond randomness in its insanity, devising complicated skeins that almost meant something, that might mean something if you were short one brain chemical or took a blow to the head or fell victim to systemic shock, and he thought there must somewhere be a race of people who knew that this was true and kept themselves addled, stunned, and shocked so as to know the many-chambered world and avoid fate's simplest snare, a reality shared by billions. He thought, too, of Arlene. Now he had gone such a curious distance from himself, could he come all the way back? Did he want to? That was the question. Did he have heart enough left in him, blood enough to tie such a simple knot? He made ready to haul up the anchor and heard a cry, a plaintive cry that planed away to a whisper, the issue of a tiny body and a metal throat. He felt a thrill run across the muscles of his chest. The qwazil. The ones who had slipped through, they must have been stranded here, and what else had been stranded, whistlers and wiccara and things he had not named and had not seen? Excitement shot through him, a familiar excitement, the excitement he had known aboard *Viator*, and he imagined the lentivirus flexing its ropy length, taking tentative flights across his brain. Several bizarre business opportunities occurred to him, not the least of which was the exploitation of the whistlers; they'd keep the place free of pests and be a true companion for a lonely hour. It astounded him he could be so easily persuaded to madness. Christ, this place was wrong forever. He weighed anchor, started up the launch, and recalled Mortensen reaching out to the engulfing fire, the image that had haunted him in the hospital. Saint Mortensen. Was he with the whistlers, preaching the gospel of *Viator* on the streets of Cape Lorraine, suffering the little children? No matter. You're either dead or in heaven, he said, his voice startling in the silence. Whichever, you're no good to me now. He did not look back until he was well out to sea and by then *Viator* had become anonymous, a black dot of solidity on a spectral shore.

At Arlene's TP, the wood-stove was going, Terry was listening to headphones, sitting in a lawn chair, feet propped on the counter, reading a magazine, and Arlene, wearing plaid jacket over her dress, was dealing a hand of solitaire. She glanced up when Wilander entered, but kept playing. With her hair pulled back, her lips firmed in an I-am-not-going-to-say-a-thing expression, she looked pretty. Pretty and a piece more, his father used to say. Terry flicked an eye toward him, making a sour show of dismissal. Wilander ignored him. He stripped off his coat and leggings, studying Arlene, staring at her for such a long time and so intensely, it seemed he was warming himself at a fire, and she could feel him staring at her, he could tell by the way she held herself, he could see the injury he had done her in the rigidity of her pose, the wounded pride, and he thought it was time he made things right, not because he owed it, but because it was what he wanted, it was all he wanted—though that certainty didn't guarantee success, not having it guaranteed failure, and he supposed that was why he had fucked up with such unflagging consistency over the years.

At last she said, noncommitally, Been out to the ship?

—I took a look. I'm back.

She slapped down a card.

He stepped around the counter and put an arm around her. Don't worry. I'm over it.

—You say don't worry, but....

He turned her to face him and said, I swear to God, I am over it. I love you.

Startled, she looked up at him and he kissed her on the mouth. She tasted of candy mints and coffee. Terry scowled at him, muttered something under his breath, went back to his magazine.

Hearing the words gave him a platform from which to say them more assuredly. I love you, he repeated. You've been taking care of me long enough.

He kissed her again, bearing her back against the counter, and felt his whole life rise up, heart to heart, with hers, in truth and in folly.

—Get a room, said Terry.